A Quiet Street in El Paso

Jim Daddio

A Wings ePress, Inc
Crime Novel

Wings ePress, Inc.

Edited by: Jeanne Smith
Copy Edited by: Joan C. Powell
Executive Editor: Jeanne Smith
Cover Artist: Trisha FitzGerald-Jung

All rights reserved

Wings ePress Books
www.wingsepress.com

Copyright © 2019 by: Jim Daddio
ISBN-13: 978-1-61309-595-9
ISBN-10: 1-61309-595-3

Published In the United States Of America

Wings ePress Inc.
3000 N. Rock Road
Newton, KS 67114

Dedication

To my wife Jill, who continues to believe in me.

* * *

One

In a large and crowed upscale shopping promenade in downtown Monterrey, Mexico a well know professor from the local college walked side by side with his wife and ten-year-old daughter. The day was clear with a bright sun and a cool breeze. The family walked slowly through the plaza enjoying the day and looking in the windows of the many shops on the street.

"Such a beautiful day," the professor said.

The professor's wife replied, "Yes. I do enjoy this time of the day to explore the shops and stop for a nice lunch."

The professor heard noises but paid little attention to the commotion. Suddenly several men ran passed them and the noise of gunfire filled the air. At first, he wasn't sure what made the sound. He figured it was fireworks. Then he heard loud screaming and without warning a bullet struck him the back. A second bullet struck his wife in the shoulder. He tumbled to the ground. His wife screamed in pain. She staggered for a minute and then slithered to the warm cement. When the paramedics arrived, the professor was dead, and his wife seriously wounded. The daughter was not hurt.

This wasn't supposed to happen in Mexico's upscale and modern city. These types of daylight attacks were supposed to happen in the border towns like Tijuana and the smaller cities in the north.

It didn't take long for the authorities to announce the attack was brought about by rival gangs trying to control the drug trade in the city. The senseless killing caused outrage from the community and pressure was brought to the local government to make hasty arrests and bring the drug cartel down. A local citizen who was well known and loved in the community had been slain and his wife wounded. It was time for action.

Within a few days, several police offices and government officials were arrested for taking bribes and withholding information. Several names were printed in the paper and all aspects of the media continued to rage a war against the corrupt government. The pressure was on to clean up the drug cartels.

~ * ~

The man known as The Captain, *El Capitan*, stood at the front door waiting for his wife and two children. He had arranged for his driver to take them to the airport. The family was taking a vacation to the coast of Spain. They would leave, and he would join them in a couple of days.

He watched as the limousine sped down the long winding driveway toward the security gate. The Captain held the opening device in his hands. As the limo approached the gate, he pressed the button on the left side and the gate slid open. His wife and two boys did not see the four-armed guards as they positioned themselves close to the ten-foot wall.

The Captain was one of the wealthiest drug lords in Mexico. He had formed one of the largest illegal drug operations in the country. Operating out of Monterrey, he had remained in background over the years. He had built an empire based on fear, police protection and force. He had also invested millions in legal business and was well known in the community for his family's involvement in the arts and charitable activities.

But it was the drug business that fueled his wealth. Over the years, he had been able to stay hidden from names being associated with the drug trade. His payments to government officials and the law enforcement agencies kept him unknown and untouchable.

That was about to change, and he knew it. The attack by a rival gang had changed everything. He had to make some type of deal because he felt certain his name would soon be mentioned. He thought maybe he could stay and fight, not only the rival gang, but with his team of lawyers he could attack those people who named him. But he had changed his mind. He would leave everything. He had connections in other towns in Mexico and the States. His legal businesses were worth millions and he had several millions in offshore bank accounts which would enable him to move out of the area and start a new drug ring.

He stood in front of the management teams from the three legal companies he owned. He explained due to ill health he would be taking a leave of absence and they would oversee the day to day operations. He didn't know how long he would be gone and encouraged them to find buyers for the companies. They assured him they could run the companies and keep them profitable. He didn't care. He knew he had to get out of Monterrey and soon.

That night he assembled the team from his drug organization. He announced, "As we know, there was an attack in a busy shopping area by, well, it appears some members of our team have broken away and decided to start a war. They didn't count on killing an innocent bystander. Or maybe it was planned that way."

"What would make you think that," one of the men asked.

"I believe they knew I wouldn't start a war. I believe they planned this and by killing a well-known and respected man in the community, the citizens would demand action from the authorities. It has already happened. I believe my name will be mentioned very soon. Some names have been already and others will also be made public. The people responsible for this attack are not known. I am. They have successfully taken over by just one act of violence.

"The police will investigate and will not be able to find the attackers. They will choose someone to be arrested. I cannot wait. I will not retaliate. I will not fight. It would bring disgrace to my family. I have made a deal already. If I leave with my family and do not return, my name will not be made public. The cost was high but necessary."

They remained silent. The Captain continued, "I have contracts in several cities in Mexico and the States. I have learned El Paso is wide open for a new drug called Black Tar or Cheese Heroin activities. I believe we can step in and in a very short time take control of the existing operation. I have outlined a plan already. I hope you will all join me."

"Are sure we can make enough money to support our families," another man asked.

"Nothing is certain. If any of you want to remain and join the outlaw gang, it is okay. I have no control over your lives or decisions. Those who do not wish to join them can come in with me. I have made you all rich and my plan will continue to do that."

Two men walked out. The others agreed to follow The Captain to Juarez.

Two

El Paso, Texas was under siege. The drug war in Juarez, Mexico had found its way across the border. There had always been a problem with illegal immigrants and drug smuggling. And to make matters worse, there was a new worry: the smuggling of guns across the border. The city fathers demanded something be done to stop the senseless crime that had filtered into their city. The latest criminal activity had become worldwide news and the city of El Paso was becoming a war zone.

The discussion in El Paso among the local police departments, the Department of Home Land Security, the FBI and the Drug Enforcement Agency was: What is the most pressing problem threatening the city of El Paso? Is it human trafficking of illegal immigrants, the cartels who control the drug trade or the thousands of businesses who hire the illegal immigrants. And what to do about gun smuggling?

They agreed most of the attention from the local law enforcement agencies continued to be the influx of illegal Mexicans crossing the border. Ever since the Department of Homeland Security had taken more of an involvement in the human trafficking problem, the local police tried to cooperate with them and with the Mexican Border

Patrol. That was evident in the raids and capture of close to a thousand illegal immigrants in the past year.

Even though those events were highly publicized, it was only a small dent in the operation of hundreds of Mexicans and U.S. citizens who engage in bringing in the illegal immigrants.

~ * ~

An officer with the DEA approached the cell of a large Mexican jail in Juarez. He could feel the buzz. Not only had his team stopped a major smuggling ring, but they had captured several members of a large group responsible for bringing in thousands of illegal Mexicans and immigrants from several Central American countries.

Bill Carson waited outside the jail. He had received a tip that several people arrested also had connections to the drug trade his team had been working on for several years. Bill was waiting for his partner, Dan Moody. When Moody arrived, they entered the cell area and were escorted to a room where two young Mexican men were waiting.

Bill and Dan pulled open the door and walked inside. Bill announced, "My name is Bill Carson, and this is Dan Moody. We are with the Drug Enforcement Agency. This is Mat Watkins. He is with the local police in El Paso. He's works hand-in-hand with Homeland Security. We understand you wanted to talk to us...you speak English?'

"Yes, sir," one of men called out.

"What are your names?"

"I am Carlos, and this is Manny."

Bill and Dan sat and faced the two men. They could hear the humming of the video recorder. Bill said, "You know this is being recorded, right?"

"Yes sir."

"Good. What is it you want to talk to us about?"

The young man spoke English without much of an accent. He started, "First, I want it known my friend and I have nothing to do with any drug cartels. We only deal with people who want to cross the border. Understood? I know this man Mat. He arrested us before."

Bill responded with a smirk, "If you say so."

The man named Carlos didn't like Bill's tone or response but continued, "We are asking for a deal."

Dan quickly responded, "We don't make deals."

Carlos said, "Too bad. You can leave now."

Bill leaned over and said, "You don't have much of an accent. Are you really a Mexican?"

The other Mexican said, "This is stupid. You're acting like an asshole and..."

Bill shouted, "Hey. Watch your mouth. You asked for us. You better have something. Wasting our time means harder times for you."

Carlos reached over and grabbed Manny's arm. He nodded. He turned back toward Bill and said, "What I am saying, and what I will give you, is big enough you should, you know, help us out here."

Bill paused for a minute, then said, "I'll tell you what. You give me something big and I'll let Mat here work with Homeland Security. Promises? I can't make any."

Carlos looked at Mat. "But you'll talk to them, right?"

Mat shrugged.

"Here it is." Carlos cleared his throat. "I'm sure you are aware of the recent murder of a professor in Monterrey. In two days, there is going to be a showdown between two drug cartels...in the States. It will be a shoot-out. Big time."

Dan stood. He walked around, placed his hands on the table and leaned close to Carlos. "You said here in the States. I don't get it. Why?"

"There is a faction in El Paso that moves the drugs once they cross the border. The local cartel there believes those responsible for that murder want to move into El Paso through Juarez. They want to make a statement, you know, send a message you can't fuck with them. They want to do it in broad daylight. Right close to the city center."

"Jesus...when?"

"Like I said it will happen in two days. And you should know that it isn't only about drugs. It's about guns...automatic weapons. Those guns come in from Mexico City. It's becoming a big business."

~ * ~

The next day there was a meeting at the El Paso police department. Beside DEA, the Police Department, representatives from the Sheriff's Department, Department of Illegal Immigration Control, the Mexican Federal Police, and Homeland Security attended the meeting.

The Mexican Federal police arranged to have a full SWAT team at the border. The sheriff agreed to do the same. It was agreed two SWAT teams in full gear, working with Homeland Security, would demonstrate a show of force to stop the attack before the massacre started. The word would be out that there had been a leak and the cartel would pull back. The plan worked. There was no shootout. The city of El Paso did not need more violence to bring unwanted attention to the already troubled city.

Three

Mat Watkins slowly tried to open his eyes as the morning sun streamed through the room's partially closed blinds. A detective with the El Paso County Police Department, Mat was facing another fierce hangover, and the simple task of opening his eyes was causing pain to rip though his brain.

Mat lay on his stomach with his head buried in the soft, lumpy pillow. He stretched out his arm and reached for a cigarette on the night-stand. He found a loose one and fumbled around for a lighter. He turned over, sat up and lit the cigarette. He took a long drag and held the smoke in as long as he could and then finally exhaled. He called out in agony. His head pounded as if someone were using a jack hammer on it. Inside, his stomach churned with a nasty sour feeling.

He looked up as a naked thin blonde walked into the bedroom. She called out, "You look like shit."

"And I feel like it, too."

She held up a cup. "Coffee?"

Mat shook his head from side to side. "I need a Coke...in a glass, warm with no ice."

The girl, Susan Weber, stage name Divine, didn't reply as she turned and trotted off into the kitchen. She was a dancer at The Pink Lady. Billed as a Gentleman's Club, it featured nude dancing and private champagne rooms used for lap dancing.

Susan returned and held out the Coke. Mat took the glass, dropped in three pain pills, and drank it down. It was his remedy to calm his aching body. Susan crawled onto the bed and slid her body on top of his. She purred, "What a fucking night. Did you take Viagra?"

Mat laughed. "Hell no. You got me so hot watching you dance at the club...I was ready as hell."

"Think you could get ready again?"

"In the shower. Come on."

~ * ~

An hour later Sue lay in Mat's arms. He leaned over and took a drag from his cigarette.

"I have to say I'm glad we hooked up. We kind of click together."

"I bet you say that to all the dancers who fuck you."

"Oh yeah, I've had hundreds."

Sue slid her head up against his chest. "I have to admit I was kind of drawn to you the first few times I saw you in the club. I liked your style. Long hair, ponytail and your I-don't-give-a-shit attitude."

"And I liked your style, too."

"You mean my tits and ass."

"You know, this would be a good time to tell me about those tits and ass. You know, who is little Sue?"

"You really want to hear about me?"

"Sure. I'm interested to know how you ended up dancing at The Pink Lady. There's something about exotic dancers and their stories that get to me. It seems you all got a story to tell."

"Heard a lot of them, hey Mat?"

"A few. Go on. Tell me about yourself."

"Well, I'm from a little town outside Columbia, South Carolina. In high school, I was Miss Everything. You know, head cheerleader, homecoming queen, May queen. Shit, I was hot. Next thing I know I'm out school and I got nothing. A few of my girlfriends had something I didn't have...school smarts. They left for college. Next thing I knew, the food processing plant closes, and my dad is out of work and Mom goes to work in the local diner. Things got really bad.

"I go from Miss Everything to Miss Nothing. All I got is a hot body and a bunch of rednecks driving around in pick-up trucks dangling their dicks. I turn eighteen and head to Atlanta. I got no job and no money. So, I see an ad for nude dancers. I give it a try. I meet another dancer who tells me the big money is in Dallas. So off we go. That didn't work out for me. Next thing I knew I was here in El Paso. I like it. I do very good at the club."

"Ever been back home?"

"Na. I heard my dad got so fucked up he left town. My mom, she moved in with her sister and well, she don't care much about me."

"Like I said. I love the stories you all have."

"And you, hotshot?"

Married twice. Divorced twice and that's all there is."

Sue sat up. "Let's fuck again."

Mat smiled. "Works for me."

~ * ~

Mat put on his black jeans, sat and pulled hard on his frog skin boots. He threw on a black Tee-shirt and wrapped his shoulder holster holding his Glock. He walked over to the closet and grabbed a black sport coat. Susan called out, "The man in black. It's a hundred fucking degrees out and you're wearing all black."

Mat shrugged, leaned over and kissed her on the lips.

"What are you going to do?"

"Pass out for a while...is that all right?"

"Stay as long as you want."

"Cool. I'll clean up before I leave."

Mat smiled and turned toward the door. Susan called out, "Hey, hotshot. Get a maid. Christ, there are a million of them in El Paso, you know."

Mat waved and found his way out the front door. He stopped for a second and felt the heat from the white sun looming lonely in the bright blue sky. He had lived in El Paso for thirty years and the heat had never bothered him. But lately the temperature had reached over one hundred degrees for days on end.

Mat was six feet-one, with long sandy colored hair that flowed just above his shoulder. He wore it in a ponytail most of the time. His body was lean and solid. He had a stern look about him and a rugged tough-guy style. He had light brown eyes and kept his blond mustache neatly trimmed.

He had joined the El Paso County Police Department a few days after he was released from the Marines. He quickly gained a reputation for being a tough, fearless police officer. He received several commendations and was promoted to detective and assigned to the team that worked with the Border Patrol arresting illegal immigrants who streamed across the border from Juarez in record numbers.

Within a few years, he was promoted again; this time to Commander of the El Paso Police Division, Illegal Immigration Control. That lasted a year. Although he kept his title, he was assigned to a new division that was formed when members of Homeland Security joined the force. His job was tracking businesses who hired illegals. It was a shit job and he knew it. But he also knew he was lucky he still was on the force.

He had recently turned thirty-five and after ten years on the force and five years doing his assigned duty, he was burnt out. With two divorces behind him and a young daughter living somewhere in Houston, he found himself drinking too much and out of control. Although he continued to do his job well, he was considered a loner, and by some, a renegade who lacked discipline and who had trouble with authority. His immediate supervisor, Captain Carl Ramirez, stood behind him because of his arrest record and his accomplishments. But he was finding it harder to support Mat lately. He had talked to him about his behavior and Mat had promised to settle down. The problem was that neither man was convinced he could. Mat loved his tequila and women.

Four

Hector Morales lived in Juarez, Mexico five miles from the Border Patrol station. He was thirty-seven, with dark black hair and a thick solid mustache. He was married with a ten-year-old son and eight-year-old daughter and a baby on the way. They lived in a small but comfortable house. He worked for a nursery and landscaping company in El Paso and had a work visa. He knew he could move to El Paso but loved his country and had no desire to leave.

Monday through Saturday Hector would drive his red pick-up truck through the border station at the same time: seven o'clock on the dot. All the guards knew Hector and he would pass through the gate with a wave and a smile. He would return every day around six and wait in the long line of tourists and fellow Mexican workers. He would inch his car forward, approach the station, and pass through without question.

Hector loved his job, his family and his life. He worked hard and was paid a decent wage. But he wasn't making enough to support his family in the manner he wanted to. He was no different than thousands of Mexican men who worked across the border.

Things had changed for Hector two years earlier. He began making the extra money he needed. Every Tuesday he smuggled in chemicals to make meth. But then that changed and now he was bringing in black tar heroin, known on the street as heroin smack or the big H. He was paid three hundred dollars a week, the extra money he needed to support his family in a better way.

He knew he would never be stopped or have his car searched by the guards. He also knew the dogs who were trained to sniff for drugs would not have enough time to find his illegal drugs and chemicals.

Still, every Tuesday Hector would get nervous. He could feel the acid drip in his stomach and his heart beat a little faster as he approached the station. Several times when he approached the gates there would be a back-up of cars leaving Juarez. He would turn off onto a side street and wait until there was an opening. He would then drive back onto the main road and go through the gate. He had never been stopped.

He followed the same routine every Tuesday. He would drive to a little café with several outside tables. He would order a coffee, a breakfast burrito and sit at the same table. He would place a black duffel bag down by his feet. Within a few minutes a man he had never met or talked to, would walk up and pick up the bag. That's all there was to it. And for this he was paid three hundred dollars a week. He would finish his breakfast and drive to work. Life was good for Hector Morales. He hoped it would never change.

Five

Fred Cummings still couldn't believe how good his life was. He sat quietly on his open patio sipping a hot cup of coffee. Every morning he would sit there shaking his head and thinking how lucky he was. He didn't even mind the heat from the morning sun. Nothing could bother him. He considered himself the happiest man in the world.

Fred was forty. He was a few inches short of six feet tall with short brown hair and brown eyes. He wore thick black glasses. He was a little overweight for his height but not considered heavy. Still, he was always trying to lose a few pounds.

It had been a wild ride for Fred over the past few years. It wasn't too long ago he was living with his parents in Houston working in the finance department of a trucking company. When a position came available for a director of finance for Strategic Electric, an electrical contractor in El Paso that specialized in acquiring government contracts to do major electrical work, Fred applied for the job. The company had received most of their revenue from winning projects for city, county and state. Fred interviewed, won the position and moved to El Paso.

In high school and college Fred was considered a nerd. He received a master's degree in finance from the University of Houston and had worked for several companies after graduation. He seldom dated and only had a few friends. This never bothered him. He enjoyed working on his computer and writing and developing financial software programs.

A few years earlier, he thought he had found the right company. He worked for them for three years and had received several promotions. But without warning the company was sold and the new company released most of their employees. He had trouble finding a job and had to move back in with his parents. Now, that was all behind him.

Fred felt the soft hands of his wife slide around his neck. She kissed his check and whispered, "Good morning."

He smiled, turned slightly and looked up at his wife. "And one to you, too."

"Hot again. I heard we're breaking all kinds of records."

Fred replied, "It's like this all over the southwest and even in the east. It's been over one hundred degrees every day."

Janice Cummings moved around and sat facing Fred. She sipped on a glass of cold orange juice. "I know I've said it a few hundred times, but it was a wonderful weekend. A lovely room right on the Gulf with a wonderful balcony and view. We have to do that more often."

Fred raised his cup. "I'll drink to that. There is nothing like a wild weekend to shake things up."

Janice laughed out loud. "And you were wild all right. Drinking, dancing, singing...and well, in the bedroom." She giggled and said, "Why, Mister Cummings, I never knew you had it in you."

He shook his head and shouted, "Neither did I."

They both laughed out loud.

Fred studied his wife as she sat across from him. He still couldn't believe he was married to such a warm and lovely lady. They had been married for a little over two years and they couldn't have been happier. Janice was thirty-six, with soft brown hair and bright green eyes. She was five-three and had a thin, firm figure. She was quiet, reserved but had a warm smile and pleasant style.

He continued to study her as she sipped her orange juice. He couldn't help but think how it had all happened. He had moved to El Paso, found a small apartment and settled into his new position. The job turned out to be unbelievable. He was a perfect fit and through his knowledge of the workings of the federal government, the company had been awarded several large contracts to upgrade the electrical systems at Fort Bliss, an Army base located outside of El Paso, and White Sands Missile Range in New Mexico. Because of his efforts, he was promoted to vice president of finance, responsible for approving the final price quotes on proposals presented to the government. He worked with the sales team on the pricing, margin and the final proposal. Because of his recommendations on format, design and competitive pricing, the company had recorded record revenues and profits. He received a bonus and was quickly recognized for his knowledge and creative thinking.

Two years earlier, two days before Mothers' Day, he walked into a small flower shop in a strip mall to order flowers to be sent to his mother. He ordered them from a very helpful and lovely sales lady. A few days later he found out she was the owner. He was impressed with her style and the way she conducted herself. He also noticed she didn't wear a wedding ring. He found the nerve to return and ask her to dinner. She accepted, and it wasn't long before they were dating, engaged and married. Soon after they found a beautiful two-story home on a quiet street in El Paso.

Janice stood and walked toward the door. "Well, I'm off. How about we have Mexican for dinner tonight?"

"That sounds good. But no tequila. I think I still have some in me from the weekend."

Their weekdays were virtually the same every day. Fred would awake, shower, grab a cup of coffee and sit on the patio. Janice would usually be up and had taken a run through a park close to their home. She would dress and be ready to go to her flower shop when Fred awoke. She would join him on the patio, drink a glass of orange juice, chat for a few minutes and then leave for work before Fred. He would then put on a shirt and tie and work for an hour in his home office before leaving. It was a routine that worked for them and Fred kept telling himself he was the luckiest man alive to be living at 11664 El Camino Real; a quiet street in El Paso.

Six

Captain Ramirez shifted through a maze of papers covering his desk. He looked up at Mat. "You look like you fell off the back of a vegetable truck...and smell like one, too."

Mat didn't reply. He waved his hand in the air and rubbed the back of his neck. The captain continued, "You know, Mat, the truth is you've been a pain in the ass ever since the Department of Homeland Security took over the immigration responsibilities down here."

"Not again. Let's not do this again."

"Damn it, Mat. I'm getting beat up because of your fucking attitude and spirit of non-cooperation. I'm tired of covering for you. Deal with it and do your job."

"They don't know shit about how to deal with the immigrants and—"

The captain interrupted, "I know...I know, okay. But we must do this. We have no choice."

Mat raised his voice. "But they won't even listen. We've been doing this since the beginning of time and these fuckers come down here and read some bullshit procedures from some bullshit manual. And...and...all this garbage about compliance and—"

He slumped down in his chair. There were a few minutes of silence. Ramirez knew Mat was right, but he also knew they had to follow the rules and regulations sent down from the department.

The captain smiled. "What do you think of the wall?"

"Right. The fuc...never mind. Yeah, like that's going to happen."

"Maybe, maybe not. But for now...did you remember you have a new partner joining you today?"

"Jesus...I forgot."

"I thought that's why you came in this morning."

"I came in because I have a lead on a company that has several, maybe as many as a couple dozen, illegal aliens working in the shop."

Ramirez showed a small amount of enthusiasm. He rose from his chair. "This is good. I mean really, really good. When your partner comes in, you can give her a briefing and get a team together and—"

Mat raised his hand. "Whoa...hold on. Did you say her? Like in female?"

The captain smiled. "Right. Betty Vasquez. She is a member of the ICE team and—"

"The what team?"

"ICE. Immigration and Customs Enforcement."

"Oh, Jesus."

"She's with the ERO Department."

"Oh, God...what the hell is that, now?"

"Enforcement and Removal...something. Hell, I don't know. Just work with her."

"Don't do this to me, Captain," Mat begged. "It's not fair. It will never work out."

"Mat, listen to me. The heat is on. Get it. You fuck this up and you'll be a crossing guard at Hamilton Elementary. This partnership has come down from the top. How many times do I have to tell you you're on everybody's radar? All the way to D.C."

Mat closed his eyes and shook his head. He didn't respond. He thought back to his last partner. A hard ass, fresh out of some secret department, who had absolutely no idea what to do or how to work the illegal immigrant problem.

Ramirez walked around from behind his desk. "She's coming down the hallway. And listen, please don't do what you did to...ah... whatever the last agent's name was."

Mat laughed. "You have to admit it was funny. That was the day I pushed him out of the car in Mexico. He was such a jerk. What was it...three, four days before he found his way back? Him and his know-it-all attitude. The guy didn't know shit."

"Cool it. She's here."

The captain opened the door and Betty Vazquez walked into the room. Mat turned and gave her a long look. She was tall, about five seven, with a trim, thin figure. She had long black hair and dark brown eyes. She wore a dark blue suit, white blouse and small black heels. He watched as she extended her hand and smiled, "Captain, my name is Betty Vasquez and it's a pleasure to meet you."

"Thank you. We were expecting you. And it's nice to meet you too."

Ramirez turned to Mat as he slid up from his chair. "And this is Mat Watkins."

Betty released her hand and extended it toward Mat. Mat hesitated for a second then reached out and grabbed her hand. She said, "Yes, my new partner. Pleasure."

Mat shook her hand, feeling her soft touch. He fumbled for words. "Right. Ah, well, welcome."

Betty slid her hand out of his grasp and said, "Thanks. I must say I've heard many things about you, Mat. And I am looking forward to working with you. I understand you can teach me a lot."

He was caught off guard with her comments. It wasn't anything like he expected. He didn't reply. There were a few minutes of awkward silence as the two gave each other the once over.

Ramirez broke the silence. "Well, it looks like you've come aboard at the right time. Mat has a lead on a company with several illegal workers."

Betty smiled broadly. "How cool is this. I'm ready to jump right in."

"Mat's going to give you a briefing and you can assemble a team and go from there."

Mat turned and walked toward the door. He didn't look back as Betty hesitated and then followed him out the door. Mat called out without turning his head. "You have a desk?"

"Yes. Upstairs."

"Upstairs? That's good. Quieter up there. Let's go up and I'll fill you in."

Seven

Mat sat in the driver seat looking over at Betty. They had parked the car a short distance from the company they were about to penetrate. They had driven from the station in silence.

Betty said, "You know this isn't standard procedure as outlined in the—"

Mat raised his hand. "Stop. I know. But we don't need S.W.A. T. We don't need to smash down the door and go inside in attack mode. I've done hundreds of these."

"Then enlighten me. I have this picture of people running everywhere; diving through windows and fleeing."

"In cases like this, the owner is usually inside. He'll line up the workers; we'll check for green cards and work visas. Then we'll move the illegal workers into the bus and drive them back to Mexico. If they have families here, they'll either work their way back to them or their families will join them in Juarez."

"And no arrests are to be made?"

"You know, it just doesn't make sense to put them in jail. We'll give the owner the time to call his attorney. We'll arrest him, take him downtown and the lawyer will be there waiting. He'll be arraigned, post bond and be back here by noon. And in a few days, he'll have a whole new group of illegal workers."

"Isn't there anything we can do? It would make more sense to throw them in jail and send a message."

"The jail is full of them. Mostly from drug arrests. I'm sorry, but the drug problem is more important than people sneaking across the border to find work. As far as I'm concerned, the immigration laws we have in this country are poorly written, outdated and don't apply to the problem we have today. They were written at the turn of the nineteenth century with only minor changes over the years."

"Well, listen to you. Political, are we?"

"Hardly. Just my opinion."

"You think Arizona has the right idea?"

"Maybe, but the new law needs some changes to make it work. And I don't want to go into what those changes are. Maybe later. For now, we need to get this over with."

Betty followed Mat toward the building as a small team of border guards waited on the bus in the alley facing the back door. She whispered, "I hope you're right about this. If not, I'll have a lot of explaining to do."

Mat stopped and looked up at the sign. 'J.B. Industries.' He opened the door and motioned for Betty to walk in. They approached a young lady sitting behind a counter. Mat asked, "Is John Baldwin in?"

"Who is asking?"

Mat flashed his badge. "Mat Watkins. El Paso County Police...and Betty Vasquez, Homeland Security."

The young lady grabbed the phone. She said, "John, the police are here." She looked up at Mat. "He'll be out in a second."

Betty leaned over, "Jesus, Mat, what the hell. He could be ushering the workers out the back...never mind. The team is there."

"He'll be here."

Within a few minutes, the door opened, and a man walked in. He announced, "I'm John Baldwin."

Mat replied, "Picture ID please."

The man held up a badge from around his neck. Mat slid closer, read it and nodded. He showed him his badge and said, "John, it has come to the attention of the El Paso Police and the Department of Homeland Security you may have illegal immigrants working for you. We have a warrant and an order to expedite this investigation. I would appreciate if we could go into your shop and check the green cards and work visas of your employees."

"You know, this is getting a little tiresome. I have a small business. I make tee-shirts and hats and other types of clothing for a few customers. You know how hard it is trying to make a living competing against the foreign companies from India, China and everywhere fucki...sorry...ah."

Betty chimed in, "Mister Baldwin. I appreciate your dilemma. But hiring illegal immigrants to work for you is, well, against the law."

"Yeah, well, it puts me in a tough situation. If I don't use them to assemble my clothes and our country doesn't do something to help me out and quit buying everything from foreign countries, I can't sell my clothes at a competitive price. I can't make a living."

"What can I say, Mister Baldwin? You may have a story to tell, but for now you're under arrest," Mat said, "Let's get this over with."

Mat and Betty watched as the thirty-some workers lined up. After checking their identifications, they arrested fourteen illegal aliens and escorted them to the bus. They walked John to the car and maneuvered him into the back seat. He said, "Thanks for not arresting them."

Betty nodded and looked over at Mat. He didn't respond as he opened the back door and Baldwin slid inside. Mat moved into the driver's seat. He looked over at Betty and said, "After we sign him in, let's grab some lunch. How about Italian?"

She smiled. "Anything but Mexican."

Eight

The man they called 'Fat Baby' sat in his limo outside of a small house on the west side of El Paso. The street, filled with debris and garbage, was lined with older run-down homes, a few of them were boarded up and empty. Fat Baby was the man in charge of the manufacturing and selling of crystal methamphetamine. It was the number one selling illegal drug, cheap, readily available and popular with college and high school students. It was also the drug of choice among the poor as well as the rich. Its ingredients included several over-the-counter medicines, hydrogen peroxide and methanol plus a few chemicals.

He was called Fat Baby because he was over six feet tall and weighed in at 300 pounds. He was black, educated and ran his drug trade like a corporation.

He was a graduate of North Texas State where he played football and received a degree in marketing. He never used drugs but realized the money that was being made selling illegal drugs. He learned the art of making meth and it wasn't long before he had developed a network of manufacturing and distributing the drug. He ran his operation with a management team overseeing all the facets of his business. The company was divided into two groups: manufacturing and selling.

Although he ran every aspect of the operation, his main responsibility was managing the finances. He spent most of his time making sure all sales were accounted for, people were paid on time and everybody who worked for him made a good living. He moved the manufacturing frequently from house to house and was always on the lookout for new places to make the drug. Nobody knew where he lived and very few people in his organization ever saw him. On occasion, he would make a visit to one of the meth houses, check out the operation and then leave. He was invisible. The narcotics bureau of the El Paso Police Department knew he was the man in charge but had never been able to get to him. He had been never been arrested. He made millions, had a team of lawyers and a network of sellers and buyers.

Fat Baby lived in a large ornate house on the El Paso Country Club. His house was surrounded by a large gated security fence and was secluded in the back by a pond on the tenth tee. There wasn't a house on either side. He bought both lots when he bought the house. It was protected by the newest and most sophisticated security system available. It was the kind of neighborhood where nobody paid attention to who lived next store or around the corner. He was never seen on the streets. If he left the compound, he would be in an oversized limo with dark windows. No one knew who lived in the house and nobody cared.

He had few, if any, competitors making and selling meth. El Paso was his territory. The other drug dealers who pushed cocaine and marijuana, let him run his operation without interference. Several new drug dealers were introducing a cheap heroin product, NS, and he knew he had to work harder to keep the meth business solid.

He was making a rare visit to one of the houses. His guards gave him a signal and he got out of the limo, walked inside and checked the area. He talked to the few members of his team and was satisfied with the work they were doing.

Fat Baby exited the meth house and slipped into the back seat of the limo. In an hour, he would be sitting in his office in his secure palace.

It was from his large office that he ran the operation. As he sat behind a large mahogany desk reviewing an Excel spread sheet on his computer, a man walked into the dark room.

"You glued to that computer screen all the time, Fat Baby, you gonna' fuck up your eyeballs, man."

"Only way I can keep up with the business. We be growin' every day."

"How many houses we got makin' the shit?"

"Ten. We got to be movin' too. I found a few new houses we can move into. You know I read that in the USA, California had over five thousand meth houses. Florida had several thousand. Texas has thousands, too. We got ten. We need more. We need more chemicals. Get Manny and tell him to come here."

"I will, boss. But I got to tell you what I be hearin' on the street."

Fat Baby looked up from the screen. He reached over and turned on a table lamp.

The man continued. "I be hearin' that a Mexican dude, Juan, he be wantin' a meetin' with you. The word is some big-time money people want a piece of our action. There's a new drug called Black Tar Mexican. It's heroin in a simple form. All they have to do is mix it with an over-the-counter cold medicine and bam, high as hell."

Fat Baby stood and rolled his large body away from the desk.

"You hear where these people are from?"

"No. Just Juan wants a sitdown. I bet that Mexican knows."

"Find out when and where. We need to act quickly on this. I don't want nobody trying to cut in on our business. Not now. We are fucking rollin' and don't need a war. That brings the law out. That's one thing we do not want. And let me know more about it."

Nine

The people who spend long hours using chemicals, common drugs and formulas to manufacture crystal methamphetamine worked quietly in a dark and boarded up garage. Carl Westbrook, a registered pharmacist, who was recently laid off, and two young college students, went about their business. The art of combining the ingredients to make the drug wasn't difficult but did require a procedure which was tedious and time consuming.

The men were working late into the night. The chemist was fast asleep. The two students sported head phones and were listening to music. The two men did not hear the sound of the door crashing to the floor. They didn't have time to react as three men dressed in black with masks covering their faces began shooting with automatic weapons and spraying the men and the room with a blast of bullets. The men twisted and turned as the rounds smashed into their bodies until they fell dead on the floor. The men continued to fire their weapons as glass and fixtures shattered. The chemist stood. It was a mistake. More bullets found him and his body tumbled to the floor.

One of the men quickly spread gasoline around the room as the other two swiftly exited the room. The lone man walked out the door, turned and again fired into the garage. They watched as it exploded and flames raged wildly. The murderous raid only took a total of five minutes. The intruders left the three dead men on the floor and hurried out of the house, having destroyed the meth manufacturing room.

~ * ~

Fat Baby sat quietly watching a late-night basketball game on TV. He looked down to see one of his three cell phones buzzing. He reached for it and pressed the talk button. The deep voice announced, "We've been hit."

"Where?"

"The garage on West Street."

"Damages?"

"Three dead and everything destroyed."

Fat Baby sat silent. He breathed deeply. He said softly, "That was a very secure facility. I have to believe someone on our team gave away the place."

"Yeah, but who?"

"I have to believe it has to do with what our Mexican friend told us. A rival gang wants to move in. They sent us a message."

"What now?"

"Call that Mexican prick and have him set up a meeting. We may have to give a little. We can't have a war. We have worked too hard in keeping the authorities off our back. Now, well, because of this, we should close down a few houses until we meet these murderers."

"I'll be in touch."

Ten

There was a certain buzz in the crowded county police station as Mat walked in. He could feel the energy. He knew something big had happened. He spotted several homicide detectives he knew talking to a couple detectives from the narcotics team. They hurried down the hall. Mat called out, "What the hell happened?"

One of the men shouted, "Bad massacre early this morning. Three dead. Shot and burned to a crisp."

"Where?"

"On the west side. One of Fat Baby's meth houses. Somebody paid a visit and tore up the place."

Mat caught up with the two detectives. He walked briskly with them down the long hallway. "What's your thoughts?"

"Somebody's sent a message to the fat man."

"You know, I just can't understand why you don't just arrest the asshole and put a dent into his operation. All I hear about is this creature they call Fat Baby."

The two men stopped. "It's hard to explain. We can't seem to get to him. Everybody knows he runs the meth business in this town, but for Christ sake, nobody's seen the fucker."

"You're kidding...right?"

"We've been after this jack-off for over two years. Yeah, we've made a few arrests. But only a few of his sellers. Hell, they've never even seen the dude. And each time we raid one of his houses, he moves to another. I bet the fucker has ten houses going right now."

"You'll get him. He'll fuck up."

"The pressure is on. We're getting heat from above. We're going all out to get this guy. And the weird thing is his problem is a small part of what's going on in El Paso. Weed is coming in from across the border in record numbers. If you hear anything, let us know."

Mat nodded as the men arrived at one of the cubicles that lined the hallway. One turned toward him and said, "I saw you a few days ago with some hot lady. She new?"

"Homeland Security...my new partner. Not my style."

"Nice. Very nice. You tap it?

The other man smiled. "Never knew you had a style. I heard if it was female and breathing, you'd be wackin' it."

"My partner...remember? Working with her is going to be hard enough as it is. Tryin' to hit it would make it worse."

"Well, if she makes a move, send her over here. We'll show her how homicide dicks do their thing."

Mat smiled and walked away.

Mat found Betty sitting in her office. He had to laugh as he approached the door. He and the rest of the officers have cubicles and she gets her own office. He put his head in the door and smiled. "Morning. Ready to go?"

"Hi...coffee first."

"Rough night, eh?" Mat said.

"I'm trying to find a place. I'm looking for a decent apartment with a short-term lease. Furnished or unfurnished. It's not easy."

"If you want I can help. I know a few people who can get you a place."

"A nice place?"

"Sure."

"Then do it. So, what is up today?"

"Let's take a ride down to the border. I know a few guards down there...on both sides. Maybe they got something they can share with us."

"And that works?"

"Come on and see. We'll stop at a little place I know and grab a coffee and something to eat. Like a hot burrito to get you going."

Betty stood and smiled. "I wonder if you know I'm Latina."

"No! I thought for sure you were Irish. You know, with that dark black hair and those deep brown eyes...and not to mention that lily white complexion."

They walked out the door and to the car. Mat turned and said, "So...Mexican, Spanish...what?"

"Cuban," Betty replied with a strong accent.

"Really. Never met anyone from Cuba."

"I am not from there. I was born in the States. My parents came over from Cuba and settled in Miami. Dad was a banker and Mom was a school-teacher. I went to the U. That would be the University of Miami. Joined the metro police right out of college. Then applied for the FBI and then, well, here I am."

"Sounds good."

"And you?"

"Finished high school in Houston. Went right into the Marines. Four years later I became a cop and, well, here I am."

"Married?"

"Twice. Both divorces. I have a daughter somewhere in Houston. I see her a few times a year. Her mother doesn't think she should get too close to me. I represent violence and stuff. Whatever. I just roll along."

Mat looked over at her. She smiled. He laughed. "What a jerk I am. Like you don't already know all this."

"Doesn't hurt to hear it from you. It's different from reading it."

"So, you probably know I've been in my share of trouble around here lately."

"I don't care much about that. I just look at your record. You may be a little off center, but your arrest record and commendations are top notch. I think I can learn from you...if you let me."

Mat smiled and drove out of the parking lot. He looked over at her and for the first time noticed she was very attractive. Her smile was genuine, and her attitude seemed sincere. He thought, *for a cop she's pretty nice looking. For a lady, she's hot stuff.*

Eleven

Fat Baby sat across from a tall and mean looking Mexican. He introduced himself as Juan...just Juan. He sat between two very large men. They were all dressed in black and each man had dark black hair and sported a thick mustache. Fat Baby had brought two of his men and he also sat between them.

The Mexican spoke first. "My friend, I am so glad you have decided to meet with me."

Fat Baby shifted in his seat. "First, I am not your friend, nor will I ever be. Secondly, I just lost three very good men and a million dollars' worth of drugs and equipment. I am very upset. And now I'm worried about the police. They have hit the streets hard. They are pushing everybody for leads. I have worked hard to keep the police away from our operation. Whoever did this doesn't understand my operation."

"I am sorry it happened. But I should tell you the people responsible for this disaster are very rich and powerful. They have made it known they want to control the lucrative drug trade in El Paso."

Fat Baby slid his body forward. "Listen to me, Juan. We have worked hard to co-exist in this city for years. I have no desire to move in on your cocaine operation and this Oxy shit. And nobody cares about the weed business. And you have stayed away from my business. Now you tell me some very powerful people want my business. Why not yours...my friend?"

Juan glared at Fat Baby. He moved both hands up onto the table and tapped his fingers on the wooden surface. "I am sure you are not going to like my answer, but I will tell you this: they are Mexicans. I am Mexican...you are not."

"So, they want to go after me because I am black. I—"

Juan interrupted. "Sorry. It is what it is. They are experienced in the new drug that is very cheap to make and sells at a good price. They know it is much cheaper to make and more profitable to sell. They have some knowledge of your operation and are ready to move into the city."

Fat Baby sat quietly for several minutes. His mind was racing. He did not want a war. He knew if he retaliated, if would mean more attention from the authorities.

Juan continued, "As you know there has been an outbreak of drug wars throughout Mexico. From Mexico City to Tijuana. The Mexican government has taken a hard stand and has begun arresting drug lords in many cities. Juarez has had very little trouble regarding the drug wars. This cartel knows that and is ready to move into the city. Just a few weeks ago in Monterrey, there was a killing of an innocent bystander by a rival gang."

"I heard about it. It was on the news."

"Yes. Very powerful leaders of the drug trade were soon to be named. One of those men knew if he stayed, his name would become known. He contacted me. This is the reason why we are here today."

"I must protect my territory. I do not want a war, but I will do what I have to do."

"There will not be a war. They are smart people. They respect your knowledge of the business. They are willing to negotiate. They have money, power and knowledge. This is what they wanted me to tell you."

"But why the attack?"

"I can't answer you. I can only guess this was their way of letting you know they are serious."

"I don't like it, but it looks like I have no choice. I will meet with these people. But you tell them if they attack again or try to take us down, I will have no choice but to go to war. I must be assured I can make the kind of money I made with meth."

"Meth is dying out as a popular drug. The Chinese are smuggling heroin into the States at a furious rate. We can offer Black Tar Mexican at a lower price and it is cheaper to make. We can own the market in the area and throughout the state. Then we can move into other states."

~ * ~

Fat Baby sat in his office. The room was dark with only a light from his cell phone. He waited for the person on the other end to answer. The ringing sound stopped, and the person answered. Fat Baby said, "Is there a chance you can find out who did this to us? They want a meeting. I cannot go into it without some knowledge of who I am dealing with. And I believe someone from our team gave them the house. I hope you can find out who it was. I'll take care of the bastard myself."

"I will do this. Give me a few days."

"Don't call this number. It will be gone after this call. I will call you in two days."

Fat Baby touched the red button and ended the call.

Twelve

The four Mexicans crept close to a long drain-pipe that stretched across the hot sand. The morning sun was slowly lifting toward the clear blue sky and the heat was already oppressive. There was an older man, maybe in his sixties, two women in their twenties and a young teenage boy. They were waiting for a truck that was to take them into El Paso. They had slipped into the U.S. side of the border and moved slowly to the place they were to meet the van.

They heard the sound of a vehicle and the old man stood. It wasn't the vehicle he expected. It was two U.S. border patrol guards in a specially equipped SUV. He slid down and warned the others. It was too late. The guards spotted the man and drove toward him. They stopped, jumped out of the vehicle and approached the old man. The teenage boy stood and began shouting at the guards in Spanish.

One of the guards shouted, "You've illegally entered the United States. Don't try to run. Drop to the ground." The other guard shouted the same command in Spanish.

The two girls stood still. The old man dropped to the ground and put his hands behind his neck. One of the guards hurried to the man and quickly grabbed his arms and thrust them to his back. He wasted little time snapping handcuffs on the old man's wrinkled wrist.

The other guard approached the two women and asked them in Spanish to lie on the ground. They dropped to their knees. The teenage boy slid behind the drain. He grabbed a large rock. He stood up and hurled the rock at one of the guards standing over the two women. The rock struck the guard in the back. The other guard removed his weapon from his holster and ran toward the boy. The boy grabbed another stone and raised his arm in a throwing motion. The guard yelled to him to put down the stone and raise his hands in the air. The young boy continued his motion when a shot echoed through the morning mist and struck the boy in the neck. The rock fell to the dirt. He stood motionless for a few seconds then tumbled to the ground.

The other guard ran to the boy and bent down. He called out, "Jesus, John, what the fuck?"

"He attacked us."

"He threw a rock. Oh, man. I think he's dead. God, there's blood all over his face and chest. You hit him in the neck."

"I was protecting us."

"We have to call this in. You know what this means. Oh man, the Mexican people are going to go crazy. And...shit."

~ * ~

Mat drove slowly down Interstate Ten. His head hurt from another night of drinking and hanging out with a couple of strippers. He had taken three of the dancers to the race track and casino across the state line in New Mexico. They drank, partied and gambled late into the night. He found a cheap motel and they engaged in an all-out sex orgy until dawn. He left the three girls asleep and found his way to the office.

Betty looked over at him and said, "You look a little pale this morning. You okay?"

"Oh, yeah. I feel just great."

"Well, your hands are shaking a little and I notice you have on the same clothes you had on yesterday."

Mat looked over and smiled. "Why so observant?"

"Training, I guess."

"Let's just say it was a long night and a longer morning. But I posted and that's all that counts."

Betty was ready to reply when her cell phone rang. She pressed the talk button. "This is Betty."

She listened quietly, nodding her head from time to time.

"I understand. We'll be there as soon as possible." She pressed the end button and turned to Mat. "How soon can we be at the border?"

"Ten, fifteen minutes. What's going on?"

"A Mexican boy was shot and killed by U.S. Border Patrol Agents."

They hurried to the car, Mat punched the gas pedal and turned on the siren. The car sped down the interstate toward the border.

The scene was chaotic when they arrived at the border station. The media had arrived, and the line of cars stretched for miles on both sides of the border. Mat steered the car down the side of the road and found his way to a parking area. They jumped out and raced to the office. Betty recognized a member of the ICE team, Randy Manning. She called out, "I just got the call. This is a mess."

"You got that right. The FBI arrived, and everyone took off to where the shooting happened."

"We need to get there."

"I'm about to leave...and who's this?" the man asked, looking at Mat.

"Mat Watkins. He's with the El Paso..."

The agent interrupted, "So you're the famous Mat Watkins. The asshole who gave Agent Ken Jameson a hard time. You won't be needed today."

Mat stepped closer to the agent. "I still have my job and my job calls for me to be involved. I do have jurisdiction in this town and know more about illegal immigration than all of you put together. If I recall, you and your team are here to support our efforts."

"You don't get it, do you? Homeland Security is running the show now. ERO is making the decisions. So, hop back in your car and go home and find something to do."

Betty said, "Take it easy Randy. I'll be responsible for him."

He replied, "I don't like it. But just don't let him get in the way."

As they drove to the scene, Mat said, "I just don't get those agents. They have little or no respect for the Mexican government. That guy Jameson didn't have a clue how to work with the police. Especially the federal police. They are tough, mean and dedicated. Get on their bad side, and act like you have all the answers, they will go out of their way to make it hard. I know."

They arrived at the scene of the shooting and were briefed on what had happened.

Mat walked back toward his car with Betty following. She said, "Sounds like the guard had a quick finger."

"He's new. I know the other guard. Good guy."

Mat walked over to the guard he knew. He said, "How'd it go down?"

"We spotted four people along that drain-pipe. They were sitting behind it. I think they were waiting for someone to pick them up. The old man there...he must have heard our vehicle and thought it was their ride. He looked up and we saw him. We drove over, and the old man and the two girls gave themselves up. The boy, he stayed behind the pipe. The next thing we knew was he fires a large boulder and hits me in the back of the head.

"My partner turns toward the kid. And the kid fires off another rock. Well, my partner pulled his weapon and shot the kid. Hit him right in the neck. Jesus, Mat, I guess he lost it. Hell, I don't know."

"What a mess. I can't wait for the backlash on this one. The FBI, Homeland Security, the Border Patrol, the Mexican police, and the family... not to mention your people...oh, wow, it's going to be a media circus."

Mat walked back to Betty. He leaned on the car and folded his arms across his chest. "No one has any answers. Damned if you do and damned if you don't."

"Are you saying the guard did the right thing?"

"No. What I am saying is this is like eternity...nobody can do anything about it, and it will never end."

Thirteen

Mat sat at an outside table sipping a cup of hot coffee. It was morning and a light rain had helped keep the heat index below one hundred. Dark clouds circled above, and thunder rumbled in the distance. It had been a couple of weeks since the news of the shooting had become a world-wide event. He felt sorry for everyone involved. His mind wandered as he waited for Betty to join him for their morning meeting.

The senseless shooting of the boy had affected him in a strange way. He had never had a reason to use his weapon. Most of the time he left his weapon in the trunk when he was on duty. He only wished there were a better way to solve the illegal immigration problem. It had become too political for his liking.

He had been drinking and gambling at a furious pace during the past few weeks. He had lost several thousand dollars at the race-track and couldn't stop. He knew he needed help, but he also knew he wasn't about to ask for it.

He sat quietly watching the people come and go. Out of the corner of his eye he noticed a man dressed in a green shirt. He read the lettering; "West End Landscaping and Nursery." He looked Mexican.

He looked beyond the man and noticed a young lady slide into one of the chairs at another table. She was very attractive and well dressed. He gave her a good look. She smiled back at him. As he watched, he noticed out of the corner of his eye the Mexican placing a black duffel bag on the ground by his feet. Within a few seconds a thin man in jeans, dark sunglasses and a baseball cap strolled past the Mexican, picked up the bag and disappeared into the parking area.

Mat knew that wasn't good. It for sure was a drop and pick up. And it usually meant drugs and/or money. He decided to make sure. He would come back to the same place each morning and see if it happened again. Something was telling him this wasn't a one-time drop. Betty arrived, and he decided not to mention what he had seen.

~ * ~

Mat went to the same cafe every day for the next week. On Tuesday, he observed the same action. It was clear to him this drop and pickup happened every Tuesday. He knew for sure this was an illegal transaction because the Mexican paid no attention to the man or showed any reaction to the missing bag.

He waited for the Mexican to finish his coffee and watched as he walked toward the parking area. Mat put his cup down and followed him. He watched as he approached a pick-up truck. When the Mexican reached for the door handle, Mat slid up behind him. He leaned over and whispered, "Don't turn around. Don't make a move. Just walk slowly over to that black SUV."

Hector Morales started to turn around. Mat grabbed his arm. "Do you understand English? I said don't turn around. Do as I say. Walk quietly. Now!"

Hector walked toward the SUV. He asked, "Who are you? Why are you doing this?"

"Open the door and get into the driver's side."

Hector followed the instructions. Mat walked around the other side, opened the passenger side door and slid in. He tossed Hector the keys. "Drive. I'll tell you where to go."

Hector grabbed the keys in mid-air, put his foot on the brake, pressed the start button and headed out of the parking lot.

"Turn right. Go two red lights and turn left. There is a park on the left. Drive into the park. Do not talk. Do not say a fucking word."

Hector's whole body shook as he looked over to see a gun pointed at him. He continued to follow the instructions and drove into the park. He looked over at Mat a few times but didn't say a word. Mat called out, "Park over there and get out. We'll sit on the bench by the table."

~ * ~

Hector sat and asked, "Can I talk now?"

"Just listen. I am a cop. Okay, get it. A police officer with the El Paso Police Department. Now, don't try to bullshit me. Because what I saw you do today for sure had to be illegal."

Hector shouted, "This is crazy. You just can't grab me off the street and force me to come with you."

"What is your name?"

Hector didn't reply. Mat raised his voice, "I asked you to tell me your name."

"I don't have to."

"Pal, listen closely. I am with the Illegal Immigration Department and—"

"I got a green card and a work permit. Take me back to my car."

"Good for you. Let me see it."

Hector knew he had to do what he was asked. He showed Mat his green card.

"Ah, Hector Morales. Very good. My name is Mat. Now, Hector, nobody puts a large bag down by their feet and doesn't get a little crazy when they realize it was taken. You didn't even look down. You didn't even reach for it. Why...because you knew some dude was going to pick it up. He walked over, picked it up and you took one last drink out of your cup, waited a few minutes and walked slowly toward the parking lot. And, very calmly I must say."

Hector could feel the heat smash through his entire body. He had been caught. Two years of doing the same thing every Tuesday and now it was over. A picture of him sitting in a jail cell and his family alone and penniless flashed through his brain. He couldn't hold back the tears.

Mat continued, "Now Hector, I have to believe it has something to do with smuggling drugs across the border or a cash payment. So tell me all about it."

"Am I under arrest? If so, take me to the station so I can call an attorney."

"Hector, Hector. I am not with the Drug Enforcement Division. My main job is to track down companies who hire illegal immigrants. I have nothing to do with drugs. Truth be told, I could care less. I drink. People do drugs. So what?"

Hector was confused. He didn't know what to do or say. He couldn't figure out what was going on.

"What are you saying?"

"Tell me everything. I am not going to arrest you. Just talk to me."

"I...I...Jesus..." Hector paused and wiped the sweat from his face. A loud clap of thunder roared above him. A light rain began to fall. Mat waved his hand in a circular motion. "Continue."

Hector ran his fingers through his dark wet hair. He shook his head. "I don't get this. What are you saying?'

"I said I wasn't going to arrest you. I know you're dropping off drugs. Come on, man, it's too obvious. I want to know what the fuck you're doing. Talk to me or face some hard shit."

"If you're not going to arrest me, then why are you doing this?"

"Hector, Hector. My man." Mat smiled. "Let me hear what you're doing and maybe we can work out a deal."

"A deal? I don't get it."

"You don't have to get it. Just start talking."

Hector stammered, "I...I don't understand but...but...I work at this nursery here in El Paso. I live in Juarez. I drive in every day except Sunday. Every Tuesday I bring in a bag filled with packages. I don't even know what is in them."

Mat interrupted, "Used to make meth...right?"

"It was. Now it has changed."

"Explain."

"It is what I told you. I used to pick up sacks of stuff. Now it is boxes. This is my first time with these heavy packages. I don't know what they are."

"And of course, you're going to tell me you don't know who you work for. And you'll probably say you never met anybody in person and each Tuesday you get in your little truck and the bag is there and a white envelope with money...right?"

Hector turned and stared at Mat. He showed a little smile. He said, "You're the cop. You have all the right answers."

"What are you paid, Hector? Tell me how much you make."

"Three hundred a week."

Mat ran his hand across his face. The rain began to fall heavier. He could feel the drops begin to pound on his head. "Let's move over under that tree."

The two men hustled over under a large oak. Mat continued, "How long have you been doing this?"

"Two years."

"Well, Hector, it's time you get a raise. Listen to me. Don't you tell anybody about this meeting. It never happened. You tell your people you need a raise. Two years and no raise, well, it's just not right. It's dangerous out there. Tell them Homeland Security is tightening things up. You need six hundred more."

"Jesus, man. They won't go for it."

"They will. We split the raise. I get a three hundred and you get three."

"You...you want in? Is that it?"

"Just do it or go to jail. You can't win, Hector. If you fuck it up and think you can get out of this by telling someone I offered you a bribe, well, it won't work. I'll deny ever meeting you. And next Tuesday morning when you drop the bag and the mark picks it up, you'll have an entire SWAT team pointing assault weapons at your head."

Hector raised his hand. "I get it. What if they don't go for it?"

"Hector, Hector...two years. You're a trusted delivery man. They need you. Trust me. They probably wonder why you haven't asked for more money by now. They don't want to lose a good man like you, Hector. Hey, you're the man...you're their man."

The men stood and started toward the SUV. Hector said, "I'm going to be late for work. I've never been late."

Mat threw his arms around the Mexican's shoulders and said, "Blame it on the storm, partner. Hey, I like the sound of that...partner."

Hector's whole body trembled as they ran through the rain. Mat called out, "See you next Tuesday...partner."

Fourteen

The loud rap music rattled through Mat's brain as he watched a young naked dancer gyrate to the loud rap music. He was very drunk. He sat quietly trying to stay awake. He dozed off for a minute and felt his head snap back and forth. He shook his head, trying to clear his brain. He slowly stood and walked toward the back of the club. One of the bouncers walked toward him. He recognized Mat and backed off. Mat slithered past him and staggered into the dressing room. He found a lounge chair and flopped down. He spread out and took a deep breath.

Several of the dancers didn't even glance at him as he moaned and groaned. He looked around for a minute and then passed out.

Divine walked into the dressing room and noticed Mat lying on the lounge. She shook her head and smiled. She walked over and bent down. She called out, "Mat. Hey, get your ass up. We're about to close."

Mat stirred but didn't open his eyes. She reached for him with the idea of shaking him but remembered the last time she did that he had reacted violently and almost knocked her head off. She called out again, "Mat, come on. Get up."

One of the bouncers walked into the dressing room. He looked over. He said, "Not again. Your pal is really beginning to piss me off. Cop or no cop, I'm about to break his ass apart."

Mat opened one eye. He looked over and said softly, "You couldn't break apart a pretzel."

"Get out and go home, okay?" The man turned and walked away.

"You able to move, Mat?" Divine asked.

He moved his body upward and rubbed his hand across his face. "How long have I been out?"

"Don't know. I've been busy. Some guy paid me a ton of cash for lap dances."

"Do I know him?"

"How the fuck would I know. Jesus, Mat. It's my job."

"I know. I know. I just wanted to know if somebody was playing us."

"Sometimes you're a little nuts, you know?"

"He still here?"

"Come on. Let it go."

"Is he still here?" Mat snapped.

"He's at the bar. You can't miss him. He's a good looking tall black man."

Mat shook his head in disgust. "It's Jamar...the bastard is playing us."

"He was not. He liked my action."

"We'll see."

Divine watched as Mat walked toward the door. She shouted, "Come on. Don't be doing something stupid. He's just a customer. That's all."

Mat knew right away the man was Jamar. He knew he was a meth dealer. What Divine didn't know was he also was Mat's key informer and, in return for information about human smuggling operations, Mat wouldn't give him up to the drug officers.

Mat walked up behind Jamar and whispered, "You be liken' my lady's action, right?"

Jamar didn't turn around. He stared straight ahead. "I don't know who your lady is, but she can't be workin' here. Ladies are too classy for you. These ladies are open for business. I dropped a few hundred on a sweet ass. That's all I know."

Mat leaned closer and whispered, "Just as long as you know that sweet ass is just for dancing and not for nothing else."

"You'd be telling me this sweet thing is your lady."

"Do I have to send you an e-mail?"

"And you're tellin' me to stay away. The lady is a dancer in a nude bar. You may own her in your bedroom, but in here's she available for anyone who wants her...and like I said, I like her action."

"Don't be foolin' with me, Jamar. Don't get too carried away. Now, tell me about the massacre."

Jamar swung his chair around. He snapped his head back. "It's some scary shit, man. I'm watchin' my ass. I can tell you that."

"Why'd they hit Fat Baby?"

"Some big-time dude wants in. That's all I know. Your boys need to find them. Could be a war."

"Could be the best thing for this town. Kill off all you drug dealers."

"Hey...hey...it's a business. That's all it is. We've be workin' this town for years. People want...we supply."

"I don't want to hear that shit."

"And why do you care? You ain't no drug cop. You be chasin' the Mexicans."

"Just curious. Hey, you got anything for me?"

"Maybe...maybe not."

"What is that supposed to mean?"

"Just don't be bustin' my ass 'cause I love that blonde ass on my lap."

"Jamar, if you want to pay for some private dancing...then pay, but don't be thinking beyond that. Get it?"

Jamar didn't answer. He changed the subject. "Two brothers. They have a plumbin' business. They got two white panel trucks. They don't got no real plumbin' business. They be movin' Mexicans for a few years. I hear they crammed so many into one of the vans a little girl died."

"Name?"

"Custom Plumbing, That's all I know."

Mat shook his head. "I'd like a meeting with Fat Baby. I…"

Jamar laughed out loud. "What? You got to be jokin', man. Nobody meets with the fat man. Hell, I've never even talked to the man."

"Tell him I got news he needs to know. Just tell him that I am now part of his team."

"I'll tell one of his boys, but I can tell you this…he won't be meetin' you face to face."

"He can call me on my private cell." Mat gave him the number and left.

~ * ~

Mat lay in bed as the dancer called Divine walked out of the bathroom. He called out, "You like that lap dancing stuff? Rubbin' up against hard dicks all night.?"

"Jesus, Mat, not again. It's my job. I made six hundred dollars tonight." She shouted, "Six hundred big ones."

"Just seems strange to me."

"First off, I don't care what it seems like to you. Secondly, it does nothing for me or to me. I just fake it and let it ride. If an asshole gets off, oh well."

Mat laughed. "I just don't get it."

"Don't hurt yourself thinking about it. Can I stay the night?"

"Sure. But I got to get up early."

"You meeting that lady cop again?"

"We got a meeting on a big one."

"I saw her. She's hot…in a different way. All dressed up and shit."

"When did you see her?"

"Last week. You two were having lunch. I didn't say anything before."

"So you think she's hot, huh?"

Susan rolled on top of Mat. "Don't be dippin' that dagger of yours in her. 'Cause I won't be letting you pop her and then you come to me thinkin' you can have me for a second pop."

"First, I don't have the slightest interest in her and secondly, I told you before. When I'm doin' one lady, I don't fuck around with any other."

"Good. 'Cause I won't be doin' it with anyone but you as long as—"

"Does this mean we got a thing going on here?"

"I guess we do. I guess we do. So, let's do it again...and again and..."

Mat laughed and pulled her close to him. She pulled herself free of his arms and slid down his body until her mouth surrounded him. He smiled and closed his eyes, hoping he could stay awake long enough to enjoy himself.

Fifteen

It had been over a month since Mat had met with Hector. The dollars he had received so far didn't sound like much, but Mat was able to hit a few horse races and win big at a Hold 'em poker game. He paid off a few gambling debts and still had a few bucks left over.

The investigation into finding the human smuggling ring Jamar had told him about was moving slowly. He had alerted the Border Patrol and Betty had also contacted several members of Homeland Security to be on the lookout for the white vans with the lettering, 'Custom Plumbing.' The vans had yet to be seen.

Mat had been disappointed Fat Baby had not called him. He also hadn't seen Jamar around either. It seemed after the massacre the drug scene had gone underground. Even the Drug Enforcement team talked about how things had slowed down.

Mat and Betty had made two small arrests and were spending most of their time trying to find the plumbing brothers. Mat sat across from Betty as they ate lunch. She said, "Thanks for finding my apartment. It's a very nice place. And reasonable, too. Hey, why not come over tonight and see the place and have a little dinner? I make a mean paella."

Mat hesitated for a second. It was the first time he could remember Betty ever talking about anything but their jobs. He tapped his fork on his plate. "I guess. If you're sure?"

"Of course I'm sure. I wouldn't have asked. I must say sometimes you amaze me. It's like you're afraid of anything social. You never talk about what you do after work or for entertainment. You are a mysterious man."

"Not much to talk about. I do my job the best I can and after that I go my own way. I guess I'm not too social."

"Well, at least come over and relax. We'll have a few margaritas and a good dinner."

~ * ~

Mat found his way to Betty's apartment, parked and walked down the long outside hallway. He found her door and rang the bell. Betty opened the door and motioned for him to come in.

He noticed right away something different about her. She was dressed in tight black pants and a loosely fitting black sweater that hung very low and open over her shoulders. Her breasts were too exposed. Either he had missed something in the way she dressed for work or she had some type of push-up bra on. Her dark hair slid over her shoulders and her behind seemed firm and tight as he followed her down the hallway. He couldn't take his eyes off her as she glided into the living room. She called out, "What do you think? Pretty nice, right?"

Mat had to laugh to himself. Was she talking about the way she looked or the way she had decorated the apartment? He replied, "Very cool. Everything fits in very nicely."

"You won't believe this, but this furniture and all this stuff is rented. I couldn't believe the choices I had. I really feel at home here."

Mat smiled, nodded his head and watched as she walked into the kitchen. He had already had several shots of tequila and was having trouble focusing on nothing but her ass. The more she moved around, the better she looked.

"I made a pitcher of my famous margaritas. I can't tell you my recipe, but you're going to love them."

She poured the drinks and they moved back into the living room. Mat took a few swigs of the drink. He smiled, "Very good. I like them on the rocks like this."

"Me, too. Now, no talk about work tonight. I figured we've been working together for over two months now and I know nothing about you except what you told me on the first day."

"There is nothing more to say. Like I said, I do my job and—"

She interrupted, "I know. But you should have some outside interests. Like a girl friend or hobbies...golf, tennis...something."

Mat couldn't keep his eyes from roaming away from her almost completely exposed breasts. He took one last drink and emptied his glass. Betty leaned over and reached for his glass. *Oh, my god,* he thought. *She's fucking beautiful.*

"Let me fill it." She grabbed the glass from his hand and jumped up from the couch. The alcohol was gaining control over his senses. He could feel the energy flow through his body. His mind was cloudy, but he felt in control. He was trying to figure out what she was doing. Was she really making a play for him? She for sure didn't know anybody in town. Maybe she was horny. Maybe she was looking for some action.

Betty ambled back into the living room. She bent over and handed him the glass. He couldn't believe what was going on. He was becoming more screwed up by the second.

She slid down on the couch. She had moved closer. She smiled and tossed her long hair back off her shoulders. It was over for Mat. He was hard as he had ever been. Something was telling him to make a move on her. She wanted him. She was giving him signals. Another side was saying no. It would make working with her more complicated. What happened if she got angry at him for making a move on her? He took a deep breath and said to himself, *fuck it. I got to do this.*

He slowly moved closer. He began to reach out for her when his cell phone blasted a loud ringing tone. They both jumped a little. Mat slid back and grabbed his phone. He didn't recognize the number. He didn't want to answer but instinctively he pushed the talk button. He announced, "This is Mat."

A deep voice said, "Someone told me you're with the El Paso Immigration Force. I hear you want to talk to me."

Mat cleared his head. He figured it had to be Fat Baby. "Is this Fat Baby?"

"Talk to me."

He stood and moved quickly out the front door. He put his hand over the phone and looked back at Betty, "I have to take this."

He closed the door and said, "I just wanted to tell you I am now part of the team."

"What the fuck are you talking about?"

"I got a partner. His name is Hector. A real nice and trustworthy Mexican delivery boy."

Fat Baby lied, "I don't know anybody by the name of Hector."

"Sure you do. He helps make your operation run. And we are now good friends. So, listen. I could give a good shit about your business. It stinks...so what? I made a nice deal with your boy, Hector. But it ain't enough." He paused for a second and said, "You listening?"

"Keep talking."

"Now, don't be messing with Hector. You got a good man there. Leave him doing his job. Something happens to him and a bad rain will fall on your parade. And you don't want me making that happen."

"Okay, but why are you telling me this?"

"'Cause I'm making peanuts. I need some action from your side."

"And why should I believe all this shit."

"It's simple. I'm having coffee and I see this Mexican drop a bag next to his feet. Then I see this shady looking dude wander over and pick it up. So, I check it out again and well..."

"I get it."

"Good. Now I need five hundred a week. Not much, is it? Just let Jamar deliver it."

"And what do I get for this generous gift giving?"

"Me."

There was silence on the other end. Fat Baby thought to himself. All the years he had taken to build his drug business he never had a bad cop on the payroll. It didn't seem like a bad idea. It was for sure a small price to pay.

"And no bullshit arrests or harassment...right?"

"Like I said, it's not my job. I won't ever help you or hurt you. I'm just along for the ride. Silence is a wonderful thing."

Fat Baby replied, "It works both ways. And so does trust. Trust me and I trust you."

The phone went dead. Mat walked back into the apartment. The mood was over. They ate a quiet dinner and he left. He couldn't help thinking about two things as he drove to the club. One, having close to three grand a month in his pocket and two, ravishing Divine all night. But then another thought popped into his mind. Goddamn Betty looked so fine. He knew she wanted him. He felt it. But what was he going to do about it? That was a question for another day... another time.

Sixteen

For as long as he could remember, Fat Baby had never felt so nervous and unsure about what was about to happen...a meeting with a cartel who wanted a piece of his action. He knew they had hit one of his manufacturing houses. They had murdered three of his people. They had the power and the money to take over his entire operation. In the years since he had taken control of the meth drug trade in El Paso, he had yet to use violence. He had done his research and checked his sales. The man was right. The meth business had fallen off. He didn't pay that much attention because he was making so much money. But he had to find out more about the new drug. How it got past him, he didn't know.

What surprised Fat Baby was the meeting was to be held in a popular Mexican restaurant in downtown El Paso. As he sat in the back of the limo, he couldn't even begin to have one idea how the meeting was going to go down. He figured the cartel was going to want a piece of the city. He didn't know how much they were going to ask for. Or maybe they wanted the whole thing. He reached over and grabbed his cell. He made a call. "You know who this is?"

Mat knew right away. "Yes."

"Time to earn your pay. Be at the Grande Mexicana restaurant in about twenty minutes. I need some backup."

"What is going on?"

"Just be there. You'll see me. I'll be the only three-hundred-pound black man sitting with a bunch of Mexicans."

Mat knew right away who he was talking about. He said, "A sitdown with the people who blew away one of your houses."

"Be discreet and watch my back."

"For a grand."

"Just be there." He tapped the end button.

~ * ~

Mat sat at the bar and watched the restaurant behind him, through the bar mirror. There were three well dressed and very business looking Mexicans sitting around a large table in the corner. There was one black man sitting between them. Mat thought to himself it was a good place to have a meeting; out in the open. The men were smiling. Fat Baby had that deer in the headlights look.

The waiter left the table after taking the lunch order. One of the Mexican men began to talk. His accent was very slight which surprised Fat Baby. "I want to thank you for showing up...alone. I have to believe you are a man of your word."

Fat Baby didn't respond. The man continued. He hardly had an accent. "First off this is a meeting that had to happen. And what happened in the past must be forgotten. Please do not dwell on it. What is important is we leave here today knowing it is over."

Again Fat Baby didn't say a word. He sat quietly, knowing he would have his turn in due time.

After a few minutes of silence one of the other men spoke. "We have to understand this meeting is about running a business, so everyone makes a profit. We both have the same goals in mind. You have a thriving, profitable business. Your reputation is well known. You know what you're doing and have accomplished a lot since taking over the operation. But your business is small. We need to talk about growing it."

Mat turned slightly around. A small table with two chairs became available beside them. He grabbed his beer and quickly found his way to the table. He could hear what they were saying. It didn't take long for him to realize the conversation sounded like a regular business meeting. The three Mexicans paid no attention to Mat as he motioned to the waiter.

Mat ordered and tried to listen to the conversation. He could only make out a few words. He laughed to himself as the men made it sound like a regular business deal.

"We are willing to make an investment in your business. Our offer is simple. Two million dollars up front and twenty-five percent share of your operation. Two of our best men will sit on the management team and have a say in the day to day operation."

Fat Baby was immediately taken back by the way the man approached the deal. He wasn't expecting anything like that. He was unprepared to even make a statement. He tried to think of something to say. He paused, took a deep breath, raised his hands and gave them a look of disbelief. He finally said, "I…I…well. I'm not sure what I get out of the deal. Two million isn't much of a buy-in."

"The two million isn't a buy-in. It's a show of good faith. What you get is us. You get protection. You get to keep a very large portion of the business. You get our experience. And we have the money and resources to double…triple our business with the supply of the Black Tar Mexican heroin. We supply the drug and with your distribution we will all make more money. Lots more money. You can keep a few meth houses, but you will be smart to phase them out. And just to let you know, we have already started. Your delivery man didn't pick up chemicals. Our man picked up our first shipment. Don't worry…your man was happy not to make the pick-up. He was paid every much to be silent."

Fat Baby listened to the inflection in the man's voice on the word 'our.' He also knew it was useless to argue or disagree. He had to give a little and then wait it out to see how it would work out, knowing he would have to keep a watchful eye on everything they did. He simply said, "I agree."

"Good. We'll need to look at your financials. We can then decide how we can spin this. After reviewing the numbers, we will be able to work out the details."

"I guess that can be arranged."

"Also, like I said, our goal is to increase production, hire more people and grow the sales numbers. We have people and the expertise to make this happen." The man pointed to one of the other men. "Marcus here is the finance man. He knows numbers. Over there is Roberto. He is in charge of production. And I will work side by side with you on the day to day business. We have the means to increase the required materials."

The food arrived. The four men ate mostly in silence. There was some chatter in Spanish. Fat Baby asked that they speak in English. They didn't respond or stop.

Mat played with his food. He knew what was happening. It was easy to figure out the men were from a very powerful drug cartel and wanted a piece of Fat Baby's drug empire. They had sent a message with the earlier massacre. The two million was sort of a peace offering. But Mat also knew it was all bullshit. They wanted it all. And would stop at nothing to take it away from Fat Baby. He wondered if Fat Baby had figured it out, too. Or was he suckered into believing by the way they carried themselves pretending to be businessmen buying into his business. Mat had a vision it wouldn't be long before Fat Baby and his manufacturing houses and his people would be taken over and destroyed. He couldn't decide if it would be worth it to have a conversation with Fat Baby. He just knew deep inside the fat man's days were numbered.

~ * ~

Mat's phone rang. He looked at the small screen. It was Fat Baby. He answered "Hey."

"You played it pretty cool. You know, sitting at the table. You hear it all."

"Some of it."

"What do you think?"

"You're asking me. I don't know a damn thing about illegal drugs."

"Don't be a jerk. I spent the last few weeks learning everything I can about you. I can't figure you out. You're highly decorated. Well respected. A fuck up and a drunk. You're like two people in one. You know your job better than anyone around. You do it better than anyone. But you take money from me and turn your eyes away from my illegal drug operation. Who the fuck are you?"

"It's none of your business who I am or what I do. Now, to answer your question. I believe you better be watching every move they make. They are bad people. I mean really bad people. That I can tell. Don't be fooled by their fancy clothes and bullshit business approach. They'll cut your throat in a second. I know you had to let them in, but you got to watch them closely."

Fat Baby didn't say a word. He held the phone close to his ear. He began to breathe heavier and quicker. He realized what Mat said made sense. He said, "I did what I had to do. There wasn't much I could say. Any thoughts on what you would do?"

"Not my problem. From what I see, they need you and your operation now. You have it running like clockwork. They know that. But I got to figure they have the people and money to do what you do. They just need time to grow into this area."

"Can you find out more about them?"

"You know, Fat Baby, you don't sound like the confident man I first talked to.

Maybe you figured it out or maybe not. It won't be long before they cut you out. Now, to answer your question. No. I can't find out who they are and even if I could, I won't. Once I open my mouth, it would take the drug boys two seconds to figure out what I'm doing. You know it's not my job. I can't help you."

"I need to put together a plan."

"The hell with a plan. Take the two million and run."

"That's funny. I made that while we were talking. Plus, I got too many people depending on me."

"You know something, Fat Baby? Maybe you're too nice of a guy to be in the drug business. Get out while you can."

"I'll think about it. Hey, by the way. Could you nose around and see if your boys from Homicide have any idea who blew my house up?"

"Fat Baby...what the hell? You just met with them."

"I know. But I have this feeling someone from my team gave up the place for cash. Maybe a lot of cash. You know, check it out from your sources and maybe you can find out who's got too much cash on their hands."

"I can't promise anything. Just give Jamar another grand. And do me a favor and keep an open mind and watch every move they make."

"I'll be doing that. Maybe I can make this work. Maybe we can all work together and do like they say...grow the business. It will mean a lot more money. I can tell you that."

"Oh yeah, more money. Sure. Be hard spending the money from six feet under."

The line went dead.

<h1 style="text-align:center">Seventeen</h1>

Mat sat on the back patio at Divine's apartment. He couldn't help thinking about the meeting he had been invited to. He knew the right thing to do would be to tell his fellow officers. But he also knew it would open him up to tons of questions. On the other hand, he didn't have the slightest idea how long it would take for the new cartel to take over Fat Baby's operation. He thought, *Why not ride along and take the five hundred a week as long as I can.*

He looked up to see Divine walk out of the patio door. "Hey, Divine. How..."

"Call me Sue, please."

Mat laughed. "Right. Sue...get me another couple shots."

She turned around and disappeared into the kitchen. She returned in a few minutes with a bottle of Patron Tequila. She said, "Here. Drink yourself crazy."

She sat and sipped a bottle of beer. The night was cool, and a slight breeze rolled across her shoulders. She looked over at Mat. "I've been doing what you asked me to do. You know...be looking around for big spenders. Now, don't get all crazy when I tell you this. That good-looking black dude...Jamar, well, he's been throwing around a lot of money lately and he's been all over me. I tell him...no touch. Just let me do my thing. He gets a little crazy."

Mat started to respond. Sue raised her hands. "Don't get huffy. I just do my job. I've told you before it's all a game."

"Well, I don't like his game."

"The other girls do. Lately he's brought in a few Mexicans who have been keeping the girls very busy. You know we don't get too many Mexicans...mainly soldiers from Fort Bliss, and a few blacks and businessmen."

Mat sat up. He smiled to himself. He knew right away these were members of the new cartel. Something wasn't right. Mat figured it was too soon for any members of Fat Baby's team to be friendly with the Mexicans. He said, "So, Jamar, how's he act around these guys?"

"You know, introducing them to everyone. Making sure we know them. They seem nice but, I don't know, there is something scary about them."

Something clicked in Mat's head. "And you're saying Jamar is throwing a lot of cash around. Right?"

"You got it, pal."

"You did good. Now let me give you a reward."

Mat knew. The man who gave him useful information about several companies using illegal workers in exchange for turning his back on his selling drugs was the man Fat Baby was looking for. He had to decide if he should call Fat Baby or let it go. In a way, Jamar had given him useful tips in the past and was delivering the cash from Fat Baby each week. But now he was pissing him off trying to make it with Sue. There was no question in Mat's mind Jamar was working his way to make a move on her. It was payback time. He figured it was only a matter of time before Jamar would flash tons of cash and try to convince her to get out of the exotic dancing business and become his lady.

Mat drove home. He called Fat Baby. He figured the information was worth a few grand. A small amount to pay for the information he wanted so badly.

He punched in Fat Baby's number from memory. It rang once. "Mat. What's up, brother?"

"Now we're brothers," Mat mumbled. "Really quick. You know our boy, Jamar."

"Delivery boy."

"Right. Well, it seems he's been hanging around The Pink Lady throwing around lots of green...and he's brought in a few Mexicans."

There was silence on the other end. Fat Baby closed his eyes and shook his head. "I'll have it checked out."

"You also need to find me a new delivery boy. And toss in two grand."

"Only if he's the mark."

"I'd bet on it."

~ * ~

It didn't take long for Fat Baby to verify Jamar had betrayed him and the team. He contacted the team leader and told him to arrange a meeting with Jamar. He was to tell Jamar he was about to get a few kicks up the ladder. He would be promoted to a team leader.

Jamar drove to a deserted warehouse east of the city. He was so excited he could hardly control the car. He figured it was about time he got recognized for his work. He drove around behind several buildings until he saw a stretch limo. "Fat Baby himself," he called out.

Jamar stopped the car next to the limo. He got out and walked around to the back. He stood silent as the large back window slowly slid down. He bent over. He smiled, "Well, look at this. It's Fat Baby himself coming to meet ol' Jamar."

Fat Baby replied quickly, "You have made a name for yourself and you are to be rewarded."

Jamar pounded his chest several times and called out, "I am the man people know and trust."

"One of the team leaders will take you to one of our houses and begin to instruct you on your new assignment. You will be in line to make a lot more money, my friend."

"Now we're talking."

Two men came up behind Jamar and motioned to him to follow them. He called out, "What about my car?"

"You won't be needing it where you're going."

It didn't take long for Jamar to figure out he had been discovered. He immediately began to make a move when the two men grabbed him and dragged him toward a waiting car. He tried to call out, but it was too late. Before he could move, a blunt instrument smashed into the side of his head and he blacked out. He didn't hear a thing as Fat Baby's limo roared down the alley.

Eighteen

Captain Ramirez studied the flyer Mat had drawn up. He looked up at Mat. "So, you want me to put this out over the wire for all departments to be on the lookout for two white vans with "Custom Plumbing" on the side."

"That'd be it."

"And you want the officers who spot the van to call you."

"You're getting it."

"I'm not crazy about doing this. You know...probable cause."

"I'm not asking for anybody to stop them. Just find out what they can about the vans and notify me."

"I'll do it, but you had better be on the mark with this one. We fuck up and we'll have the brass on our ass."

"Nice rhyme." Mat left the office.

Two weeks later Mat got a call two officers had seen one of the vans and observed it parking at an apartment complex in Southeast El Paso...Sunrise View Apartments. He also found out there was no company called, "Custom Plumbing."

Mat called Betty. "Meet me in an hour on South Central Avenue. There is an abandoned gas station on the corner. And guess what? You get to call in fire power. I found the vans."

"I'll get on it."

Mat watched as a SWAT armored vehicle pulled in back of the station. Betty drove in behind the vehicle and stopped. She slid out of the car and walked over to Mat. He spoke first. "The two vans are still there. I didn't want to do anything until you and your squad arrived. We need a strategy."

"Any thoughts?"

"I was going to go to the manager's office and find out what apartment the brothers lived in. But I thought he could be involved in some way and give them a heads up. It might be best to wait them out. They have to come out sometime. The vans are parked at the end of the covered lot. I don't think we want a wild shootout. I just want to be careful."

"I wish we knew more about these two guys. I agree we don't need a shootout. But I don't like the idea of waiting around all day and night."

"I know. But we don't have many other options. They have to come out of their place sometime."

"You know, Mat, everything we're doing here is unauthorized. We don't have probable cause. Shit, we don't even know if these guys are the ones we're looking for. We're going on a tip. Mat, I..."

"It's what I do. We have a job. And it's a simple one. Stop illegal immigrants from coming across the border and mainly stopping those who smuggle them in. We should take chances some time. I've done this before. You should trust me. Most of these smugglers are not hardened criminals. To them it's another way to make money. Of all the arrests I've made, I have yet to use my weapon. When they come out of their apartment, I guarantee you if we approach them, they'll come with us peacefully. Hey, we've made three arrests since you came aboard and—"

"I know. I know. Okay. But something's a little different in the way you're acting."

"What's that?"

"Asking for a SWAT team, ah, Mister No-violence."

"I wanted to make you happy."

"I'm not buying it. You got a bad feeling, don't you?"

"Let's just say a little backup wouldn't hurt, just in case things go haywire."

"You're contradicting yourself...and that worries me."

The afternoon dragged on. The SWAT team was getting edgy. They expected action. Sitting around was not their strong point. Mat dozed, and Betty stayed focused on the vans. It was close to five when the two men walked into the parking area. Betty grabbed Mat's arm. "Mat, two men. Wake up."

Mat snapped to attention. He wiped his hands across his face, opened the door and slid out. Betty got out of the car on the other side. Mat watched as the two men approached the van. He called out, "Let's go."

Betty followed him as he ran toward the two men. One of the men started to open the van door when Mat yelled loudly, "Hey, you there. I need to talk to you for a minute."

The man turned toward Mat. The other man stopped and turned toward him. Mat and Betty came closer. Mat identified himself, "Mat Watkins, El Paso Police. This is..."

Before he could finish, both men turned and began running down the street. Mat didn't hesitate and took off after them. Betty wasn't sure what to do. She turned toward the officer in charge of the SWAT team and motioned for them to disperse.

Mat watched as one of the men turned and sprinted between the apartment buildings. The other man dove over a row of hedges and came up running through an open field. Mat motioned for Betty to follow the man who had run between the buildings. Mat charged after the other. He turned to see several members of the SWAT team racing toward him. He pointed them in the direction of Betty.

Mat continued to run onto the open field. For a second, he lost sight of the man. Then out from behind a large bush the man appeared and before Mat could react, the man was pointing a handgun in his direction. Mat heard gunfire and instinctively dove to the ground and rolled several times.

Mat called out, "What the hell? What are you doing? I just want to talk to you and…"

Another bullet whizzed past him. Mat located a small tree and crawled behind it. He looked up to see several members of the SWAT team racing toward the man. Mat figured they had heard the shot.

That was exactly what Mat didn't want…a public shootout. He knew for sure some bystander had heard the shots and had already called 911. Which of course meant the media. With all the danger and excitement going on about him, all he could think of was the media attention and explaining all this to his boss. Not to mention the paperwork he would have to fill out.

As soon as the man spotted the SWAT team, he threw his weapon in the air and raised his hands high above his head. Mat ran toward him. He called out, "What the hell was that for? Jesus, you shot at me. What a jerk."

A member of the SWAT team instructed the man to lie flat on the ground. He thrust his hands behind his back and wrapped handcuffs around the man's wrist. Mat asked, "What is your name?"

The replied quickly, "Henry Woods."

"Well, Henry, you are under arrest for many things. But mainly for shooting at a police officer. I'm going to read you your rights. Even though you lost them when you shot…never mind."

Mat read him the Miranda Act Rights while the other officer pulled the man to his feet. When he was finished, he said to him. "See, I don't get this. You and your brother smuggle illegal immigrants, that would be Mexicans, into the States. Big deal. All you had to do when I approached you was stand still, let me talk, lie to me and when I was finished, ask to see your attorney. Now, you're fucked. Smuggling is the least of your worries."

The man remained silent. Mat drew closer to him and said, "Aren't you going to say anything?"

"My attorney will talk for me."

"Cool. And after the CSI unit goes over the two vans and finds enough evidence about…"

Betty came running up. She heard Mat ramble on. She stepped in front of him and looked at Woods. "He's babbling. He does that when he gets shot at."

Mat said, "You get the other man?"

"He's already in the vehicle."

"It go down easy?"

"He kind of was trapped in front of a wall. I was about to fire a round over his head when he turned, saw my weapon and fell to the ground."

"He have a weapon on him?"

"No."

"Now why didn't I chase after the one with the weapon? I don't like being shot at."

"And of course, you didn't have your weapon on you. Yeah, mister-every-arrest-I-make-goes-down-easy. Better wake up, solider, and carry your weapon. You may have to protect yourself...again."

They watched as the officer pushed the man toward the vehicle. They looked up to see two black and white police cars approaching. Mat said, "As I figured, someone called nine-nine-one and, oh look, here comes the news crew from one of the TV stations."

Betty laughed and said, "Looks like it's going to be another media circus."

"Hey, I got a great idea. You handle this. You know, Homeland Security tracks down and captures two human traffickers. You'll look great and you'll be on TV and all that good stuff."

Before she could react, Mat headed for the SWAT vehicle. He pounded on the door and when it opened, jumped in. He couldn't hear Betty screaming obscenities at him. She then turned toward the TV crew as they moved closer. For a second, she thought to herself, *this could be cool.*

Nineteen

It had been a few months since Fat Baby had his first meeting with the Mexican drug cartel. He continued to have several meetings with them, and the transition was going smoothly. As far as he was concerned, he was impressed with their energy, knowledge and the fact he actually was making more money.

The cartel brought in more of the new drug and there were buyers everywhere. It was an open market and the money was pouring in. Whatever the drug was, Fat Baby didn't know about or care to learn about it. His meth business was slowing down, but he wasn't concerned.

Even though he was making more money, he *was* concerned about the two million promised to him. He had hesitated to mention it because it would make him sound cheap.

Fat Baby stood on his patio and watched as the clear dark sky flickered with a million stars. He took a long drink of his single malt scotch, swirled it around in his mouth and then swallowed slowly. One of his several cell phones rang. He reached for it, touched the answer button and announced, "Talk."

The voice on the other said, "It has been arranged. The money will be delivered by one of your men. Someone we have learned has proven to be very trustworthy. You know him as Hector. The money will be delivered next Tuesday. Where do you want the money delivered?"

Fat Baby thought for a second. He wanted to make sure if something happened the money in no way would be tied to him. He quickly came up with a plan. He would have the money delivered to his accountant, a man he knew as Charlie.

He fumbled through some of the papers on his desk. He found Charlie's address, 11646 El Camino Real and pressed the red button on his phone. At the other end, the phone went dead.

~ * ~

Mat was drunk and feeling depressed. He had gotten himself into a situation he didn't care for. Never in his wildest dreams could he have imagined when he made a deal with Fat Baby it would turn out this way.

Fat Baby was abusing the deal they made. He had begun asking Mat to do odd jobs for him. At first they were small chores; like watching a deal that was going down or riding by a few meth houses to check on them. All this for a grand, sometimes more.

Mat wanted to stop the deal, but he knew he was in too deep. The money was making him crazy. He was drinking, partying and gambling at a furious pace.

The only thing keeping him going was he could continue to do his work. He had gained Betty's trust and together they were able to make several large arrests. She began to like the publicity and notoriety the press was giving her. Betty had become somewhat of a celebrity.

Mat sat at an outside table on a warm evening having dinner with Betty. She said, "I think I'll write a book about my...our successes."

"Don't use my real name."

Betty laughed. "I'll call you Preston Parker...cool, huh?"

"Sounds like you've already started it."

"I was a journalism major in college, you know. My first job was with the *Miami Herald*. But a law enforcement career came calling."

"Sounds like you're kind of liking the media attention."

Betty laughed again. "Hardly. Hey, you could get in on this action, you know."

"No way. Not going to happen. I love the fact Homeland Security is getting all the attention. That lets me do my job and stay in the background. You go, girl."

"But Mat, we're a team. And you're the team leader. You're missing all good stuff."

"Just call me Preston."

Betty threw her head back and laughed out loud. She could hardly catch her breath. She leaned over and whispered, "And you're missing something else."

"And that would be?"

"Me."

Mat was caught totally off guard. His fork slipped out of his hand. He looked up to see a smile on her face like he'd never seen. He motioned with his hand and said, "Me and you...you and me. A young beautiful woman and a washed up old drunk. Are you drunk?"

"It's time, Mat. Pay the check and let's get out of here."

"Waiter!"

~ * ~

"You slept with her, didn't you? You slept with that lady cop. I know it. I can tell by looking at you. Goddamn you, Mat."

"We were both drunk. She was all over me. I got caught up in the moment."

"Jesus, I knew you would. I saw her. She's young and hot."

"Not as young and hot as you."

"What the hell does is that supposed to mean?"

"Hell, I don't know. Listen, just listen," Mat took a deep breath. "It is not going to happen again. It was awkward at best."

Sue sat quietly, pouting. She closed her eyes and shook her head. "You know I get asked a hundred times a night. But I won't do it because it will come down to money...and I ain't no whore. I'm a dancer. An entertainer. But damn, you said when you were with one girl you wouldn't..."

"I know. I know what I said. It's still me and you. It wasn't that good anyway. Like I said, it won't happen again. I can assure you of that. I fucked up, but I don't want to lose you. Okay?"

Sue looked over at him. "You got anything left in that tank to prove it?"

"Get in the shower and I'll show you."

Sue walked toward the bathroom. "What is it with you and the shower?" She turned around. "You do it with her in the shower?"

"On the floor. Now move it. I'm getting a boner already."

Twenty

As far as Mat was concerned, everything was a bunch of bullshit. First off, he loved his job and had done it well for years. Then along came a new group of bureaucrats from the Immigration and Naturalization office. They came aboard and started making changes and driving him crazy. Then the FBI showed up. He never understood what they were doing. When he finally made it a point to teach the new officers the right way to handle the illegal parade of people crossing the border, in came Homeland Security with their rules and procedures.

In his mind, nobody knew who was in charge of what. What had bothered him most of all was the fact they didn't treat the Mexican police and border patrol with much respect. They believed all of them were taking bribes and turning their heads instead of making arrests. Mat knew that wasn't true. It had taken him years to build up a good working relationship with the Mexican teams. They wanted to control the flow of illegal immigrants as badly as his team.

Mat walked toward his favorite bar on the U.S. side of the border outside of mid-town El Paso. He had made several Mexican friends over the years and was always welcome there. He entered the bar and nodded to the bartender. The man smiled and poured him a shot of tequila. He watched as Mat gulped it down and waited for him to slam the glass on the table. He refilled it quickly.

The bartender pointed to a man sitting alone at a corner table. He whispered, "Good timing, my friend, this man has asked for you several times."

Mat didn't turn to look at him. He asked, "Do you know him?"

"No, *señor*. He is new around here. He is Mexican."

"And do you have any idea why he asks for me?"

"Again, no."

"Thanks."

Mat grabbed the bottle and a glass and headed toward the man. He stood there looking down at him. He was short, with long black hair and a full mustache. He wore a ball cap.

"I am Mat. You have asked around about me."

The man pointed to a chair. Mat sat down, poured the man a shot and one for himself. They both drank at the same time. The man said in poor English, "I have asked for you because I have heard you're an honorable man. A policeman, but a man who can be trusted."

Mat didn't reply. He waited for the man to continue. "I have information I want to give you. I will not tell you my name or how I got this information. I will remain, as you would say, anonymous."

"No argument from me. Continue."

"I have information that comes from my heart. I have been saddened by the death of my granddaughter. She has died trying to come to this country. Your country. She died in the collapse of a tunnel. A very secret tunnel."

"I'm sorry for your loss." Mat poured two more shots. Again, the men drank together.

The man continued. "It is very hard for me. I love my Mexico and have done well but I understand why so many people want to come to the States. I know by telling you this I will kill the dreams of so many people. But I also have to do my part to stop this insanity."

Mat noticed even though the man's English at times was very broken, his choice of words established him as being very educated. Mat was also impressed with his poise.

"I understand," Mat said. "I, too, wish I could do more."

"I will take you to the tunnel. I cannot tell you when. But it will be soon."

"Okay."

"How will you handle this?"

"I have a few questions to ask. The tunnel will be heavily guarded. Will we be able to get close?"

"I have been lucky to find the end of the tunnel on this side."

"Very good."

"I must tell you that I am surprised the tunnel has been in operation for some time and the authorities have not found it. It is a very sophisticated tunnel. It is well lit with air ducts and is well fortified. There is a track with wheeled carriers to bring the drugs in. Now they are using it to bring in people. There was a collapse. Some blame it on a small tremor. Or maybe a poorly constructed area. That is not important. Your people must be blind...and my people, too."

"You asked how I will handle it. I want to see it first. Then I should contact my authorities and they will decide what to do."

"I see. Then it is settled. Please contact the bartender by the end of the week. He will have information on when and where we will meet."

The man stood and walked slowly out the door. Mat sat for a while, drank a few more shots and headed to The Pink Lady. It was payoff time and he was to meet the new man who would deliver the money. He knew it wouldn't be Jamar. He had not been seen or heard from Jamar all week. Mat knew Fat Baby had taken care of him. How? He didn't care.

Twenty-one

Betty returned to El Paso after a week-long meeting and briefing in Washington. She had given her superiors a favorable report on Mat. She was pleased with his efforts, procedures and work habits. She told them at times his methods were unconventional, but he always got the job done.

She arrived at her apartment and immediately called Mat. He answered on the first ring. "Mat, I'm back from D.C. What's going on?"

"Welcome back. And good timing. I have a lead on a tunnel."

Betty jumped to attention. "That's terrific. Where? When are we going?"

"Whoa. Slow down. This must be done a certain way. My source is very nervous about this. He is taking us to the end of the tunnel here in El Paso. And please do not tell anybody from your team. Let's check it out first."

"Mat you know I can't do that. I have—"

Mat cut her off. "Never mind. I'll take this one alone."

Betty frowned. "You're killing me...you know."

"It has to be checked out first. You must trust me on this. The information is too sketchy."

She gave in. "When?"

"Be ready in an hour. I'll pick you up and brief you then."

Betty walked in circles in front of her apartment waiting for Mat. This was the biggest opportunity she'd had since joining the team. If they pulled this off, she would be in line for a citation and maybe a promotion.

She jumped and looked at every car that passed by. She was excited and nervous at the same time. She called out softly, "Come on. Where are you, Mat?"

Mat pulled into the parking lot. Betty waved and jogged toward the car. Mat had to slam on the brakes to avoid hitting her. She opened the door and bounced into the seat. "A little excited, are we?" Mat asked.

"I'm been waiting out here for an hour."

"I said four. It's ten till."

"I know, I know. I was itchy, so I came outside. So enlighten me."

"First, as you know, this type of operation is important to me. I've been on several wild goose chases looking for tunnels. A few years ago, one of our men found one and was killed. And since I did get the tip, I want us to check it out first before we start running around telling everybody about it."

"How did you hear about it?"

"There is a little bar downtown where the patrons are mostly Mexicans. I know the people who own it, and everyone knows me."

Betty stopped him. "And why haven't you taken me there? We are partners, you know."

Mat stuttered. "I...well...hell, it's just a bar. I haven't been there in a while."

"Take me one day."

"Right. Here's the deal. I stopped in last week and the bartender told me that a guy sitting at one of the tables was in several times asking about me. He wanted to talk to me. I sat with him and he tells me a sad story about how his granddaughter was in the tunnel and part of it collapsed and she was killed."

"Oh, that is so sad. I just didn't expect all this death. First, the boy is shot by a border guard. Then we learn a little girl dies in a van. And now this."

Mat looked over. "Reality, Betty. What can I say?"

"So, go on."

"I went back to the bar yesterday and got the message I was to meet the man today at an industrial park outside of town. I'm not familiar with the area. It's called Park East Industrial Complex. We should be there in about fifteen minutes."

They drove in silence for a few miles. Betty looked over and said, "Aren't you interested in how the briefing went in Washington?"

"Should I be?"

"Somewhat. There was a discussion about you and your team."

"And?"

"Well, when you come over tonight, I will brief you. You are coming over, right?"

Mat felt flustered. He stammered, "Right...I mean yes...we'll see...maybe."

"Jesus, Mat. Take it easy. You look a little flushed. So it happened. It just happened. Okay. Damn."

Mat pulled into the industrial area and noticed a long stream of lowrise buildings. Some of them were occupied, with the names of the companies over the door. He drove slowly looking for the man, who had told him he would be in a white Lincoln. Mat drove close to the end of the parking lot when he saw a white car sitting alone. There was a man inside. He pulled next to the car.

The man got out of his car and walked toward the passenger's side. He stopped when he saw Betty sitting in the front seat. He looked through the windshield at Mat. Mat saw the look on his face and motioned for the man to come to his side of the car. He touched the button and the window slid down.

"What is that lady doing here?" the man asked.

"My partner. Get in the back."

"You were to come alone."

"I never said that. Now get the fuck in the back."

The man opened the door, bent down and slid into the back seat. Mat said, "This is Betty. Very capable and very tough."

The man nodded. Betty said something in Spanish and the man nodded again. Mat turned around and said, "It's your show."

The man appeared nervous and Mat could see the sweat rolling down his face. The man spoke softly, "When you first drove in here, there are two large warehouses. The second one does not have a name on it. The tunnel ends in the basement of that building. But what is very strange is there are no visible steps that lead down. The steps are behind a fake wall."

Mat looked over at Betty. He had nothing to say. He was hoping Betty would ask a question or two. She stared straight ahead.

The man continued. "It looks very quiet. But I have been told there are always several armed men inside. I also have been told the tunnel is used mainly to bring drugs across the border. As I said, lately they have been using it to bring in people."

"Anything else?" Mat asked.

"I cannot think of anything. I have told you all I know. Now it is up to you to do whatever you do."

"Thank you, sir." Mat said.

The man opened the door and slammed it shut. He leaned over the open front window. "Close it down and bring to justice those who have killed my granddaughter for profit." He turned and walked away.

"Let's get out of here," Mat said "I don't like sitting here. We can talk about this back at the office."

Mat started the car and began to pull out of the parking space when he saw a white truck with some notations of a moving company painted on the side. Mat stopped for a second when he saw the van stop in front of the warehouse the man had pointed out. Two men got out of the truck and went inside. The truck continued down the street and turned at the end of the row of warehouses.

"There must be a docking station in the back."

"You're not thinking of doing anything now, are you?"

"We have to see what's going on back there."

"No. No we don't. Let's report this and get the ICE team in here and follow procedures."

Mat smiled and turned the car toward the end of the warehouses. He pulled up just enough to see the truck. It had stopped and backed up to the building. The driver got out and opened the back of the truck and threw several large moving type boxes on the ground. Several men came out of the building carrying large brown duffel bags.

"Marijuana," Mat said.

"You think?"

"Oh, yeah. A shipment must have just come in. Look, they're putting the weed into the moving boxes."

They watched as the men finished packing the boxes and loading them into the truck. They waited for the driver to return to the truck.

Mat turned toward Betty, "How fast can you get your team out here?"

"Now? You want to do something now?"

"Right this fucking second. Call someone. I'm calling our drug enforcement team. Might as well have the whole gang here."

Betty punched a few numbers into her cell. "Code Red." Mat handed her a piece of paper. "Park East Industrial Park Complex. Warehouse. Illegal drugs being brought into the U.S. and a possible tunnel."

Mat called his boss. "Hey, get a full SWAT team out to Park East Industrial Park Complex. Heavily armed and dangerous drug dealers. And a tunnel from Mexico. The ICE team is on their way."

Betty cried out, "Oh man, without a federal warrant?"

"Probable cause. We witnessed a possible crime and called it in."

"But why were we here?"

Mat laughed. He gave her a funny look. "We wanted to be alone."

"Yeah, right. What turned out to be a good thing could get us in trouble. Why couldn't we have observed? Reported. Got a warrant. And came out here with guns a blazin'. No. Not you."

"We still would have had to explain what we were doing here."

"Sometimes a tip gets what we want."

"See, you're getting this already."

They sat for in silence for a few minutes and observed the truck and warehouse. After several minutes, Betty said, "You would think they would pack up and go. It could be a mistake, just sitting around here."

"I have a feeling they are waiting for something...or people from Mexico."

"You could be right. I'm hoping that's not the case. If they have immigrants coming in, it could turn into a hostage situation."

"I was thinking the same thing."

Betty looked at him. "Damn you, Mat! You and your John Wayne ways...get to be a hero now. Shit!"

Twenty-two

Betty drove the car outside the entrance to the industrial park. Mat had to laugh to himself. All the times he had made arrests over the past several years he never had to use his weapon or encountered a dangerous situation. He was now faced with the possibility of another shootout.

Mat circled his finger around the trigger of his Glock. He was an excellent shot and always scored high during his mandatory yearly trips to the firing ranges. He just didn't like the fact he might have to use it.

Betty parked the car just to the right of the main entrance. She was waiting for backup to arrive. It didn't take long. The first team to arrive were the officers from the Drug Enforcement Agency who had teamed up with the local El Paso drug enforcement officers. She was about to brief them on the situation when the team from ICE arrived in full force.

Betty counted a total of ten officers. Some of the SWAT team were dressed in full protective gear. She began her brief. "Based on a very reliable source, my partner and I were able to locate a possible tunnel from Juarez that ends in a warehouse located in this complex. We observed a large truck enter the area and park in the rear of the warehouse and saw several large boxes being loaded in the truck. We believe based on the size and shape of the boxes, the substance in question is illegal drugs."

One of men called out. "How did you determine that?"

"We observed two men place bags into several large boxes and believe the bags were filled with marijuana." She waited for a response. After a few minutes, she continued. "We also have learned there are armed guards inside the building. We know there is a false wall that hides a door leading to stairs going down to the basement and the end of the tunnel. We also feel the reason why the truck did not leave immediately after being loaded is because they are waiting for illegal immigrants coming through the tunnel. If this is true, it could lead to a hostage situation. We need to move quickly to avoid this."

The officer in charge of the ICE team stepped forward. "We need to formulate a plan on how to approach the situation. I'll need to speak to the man in charge of the drug enforcement unit."

Betty listened in as they formulated the plan. It was decided the DEA unit would strike from the front entrance while the SWAT team and the command vehicle would be positioned at the back entrance.

She called Mat on her cell. "Mat, your drug unit is going into the building from the front. I am going to join the ICE team which will be positioned in the back."

"I'll move around to the front. Nothing has changed but we should move now."

"We are. We're moving out."

Mat stayed low and trotted around to the front of the row of buildings. He saw the black SUV drive up to the front of the building. He ran toward it while five members of the team got out of the SUV. Two were holding a battering ram. Mat joined them, nodded his head and waited for the commander to give the signal. When the call came in, ICE was positioned at the loading dock next to the truck. When the command was given, the two men charged the door and smashed it open.

The officers charged into the room yelling and screaming. They commanded everyone to fall to the ground. About that time all hell broke loose. Two men were sitting at a long table. When the door caved in and the yelling started, they were caught off guard. One of the men reached across the table for his automatic weapon.

One of the police officers called out, "Don't do it. Don't touch the weapon." The man continued to grab the weapon and started to turn it toward the officer. The officer fired his weapon and struck the man in the shoulder. The gun fell back on the table and the man fell to the ground screaming in pain. The officer quickly moved toward him, grabbed the large weapon and shoved his hand-gun into the back of the man. He didn't try to move.

The other man yelled something in Spanish, fell to the floor and scrambled toward the back. He stopped suddenly when he felt the weapon's cold steel barrel touching the back of his neck. The officer quickly pulled his arms around his back and handcuffed him.

When Mat heard a door opening, he turned around. A man and a woman entered the room. Without hesitation Mat pointed his weapon and shouted, "Don't move. Hit the ground...hit the ground now!"

The two people fell to their knees and then slowly slid onto the floor. Another officer came forward and called out, "Hands behind your heads."

Within a few minutes, it was over. Mat walked over to the two people lying on the floor. "Where is the false wall and the door to the basement?"

The woman pointed to two large gray filing cabinets against a wall. Mat and several officers moved quickly and pushed them aside. There was nothing different about the wall. Mat called out, "What is this? Do we need to knock it down?"

Nobody responded. He walked over to the man and woman. Before he could ask them again, the woman said softly, "Part of the wall is on rollers. You can't see them. You have to push on the wall and then slide it."

Mat quickly walked back to the wall and two of the officers joined him. They pushed the wall and it moved slightly back. They pushed it to the right and the wall moved to the side. They spotted the reported set of stairs.

The call was made to the team behind the building. The vehicle moved toward the truck and five members of the team exited the vehicle and ran toward the truck. The truck had been parked backwards against the large open delivery door and two men were sitting on the dock. They froze in fear as the team approached them.

Two fully armed men inside the building walked out onto the loading dock. They saw the SWAT team and made a fatal mistake. They began yelling and opened fire on the SWAT team. The team returned the fire and two men were splattered with bullets and fell to the ground.

Mat and the other officers ran down the steps. They located the opening to the tunnel. It looked to be about six feet high and four feet wide. Mat radioed for Betty and suggested she bring two members of the ICE team to come into the building.

The leader turned toward Mat. "I am concerned about the tunnel. We don't know where it begins, therefore we cannot have our team in position in Mexico."

Within a few minutes, Betty and her team entered the building and spotted the opening. They raced down the stairs.

Mat greeted them with…"Well, this is it."

"What now," Betty asked.

"First, there are several people upstairs. Question them and find out what they know. If I could, I would like to make a suggestion. I wouldn't send anybody in there until we find out the location of the entrance to the tunnel on the Mexican side. We don't know how long it is or if there is anybody coming this way. It could prove to be dangerous for everyone."

Betty stood next to them. She said, "I can do that. I'll go back upstairs and interview the people."

An ambulance, a complete medical team and a fire truck arrived on the scene followed by the news teams from the local television stations and newspapers. Betty returned and gave the information she had obtained from the woman. She said, "She didn't say much. She calls herself the office manager. She claims she knows nothing."

Mat and Betty stood by the tunnel. She said, "Want to go in and take a look around?"

"A tunnel is a tunnel."

"Looks very well made from this end."

"Okay. But we can't go far."

Betty led the way. She bent down and took small steps into the tunnel. Mat followed. She stopped when she heard a noise. She held up a finger to her lips, then whispered, "I think I hear something. Yes, it sounds like voices."

She motioned for Mat to back up. They exited the tunnel. She turned toward the leader. "I think we have people coming this way."

Mat said, "I don't think they're going to like the welcoming committee."

They hunkered down to wait.

Ten minutes later a man exited the tunnel, stood and looked around. As soon as he saw them, he didn't hesitate. He dropped his weapon and threw his hands high in the air. Two officers grabbed the man and pulled him to the side to handcuff him. Within in a few minutes several Mexican people crawled out of the tunnel.

Mat jumped up, shouting, "*Alto...parada!*"

The sting was over.

Twenty-three

Mat stood at the entrance to the tunnel. He looked over at Betty. "Ready?"

"Huh? Ready for what?"

"We're going in. To the other side."

"Do you think it's a good idea?"

"Here's the plan. We need two of your best men. When we get to the other side we'll observe and figure out where it begins...or ends. If we can get a GPS tracing, we'll call the Mexican authorities and they'll join us. I have a good contact I can trust."

"Let me talk to my supervisor," Betty said.

"Do it quickly."

Within a few minutes, Betty, Mat and two heavily armed officers from the DEA moved through the tunnel which was well constructed with bright lights and a railroad type track.

"Look at these tracks. They can slide the drugs in a cart along this tunnel every quickly."

Betty didn't respond. An empty cart sat on the tracks. As they crept closer. Mat whispered, "This is it." As they approached the end of the tracks, there were two spotlights shining on a large wooden door.

Mat approached the door and pulled up a large wooden rod. He said, "Looks like it slides."

Betty moved next to him. She looked over her shoulder to the two officers. She took a deep breath. "Well, let's do this."

Mat slid the door to the right. A clump of bushes fell into the opening. The two officers moved toward the door and began to pull back the bushes. A ray of light began to shine through. They pushed and walked into the area. Mat heard one of the officers yell, "Drop your weapons and fall to the ground. Do it now."

Mat and Betty scrambled through the bushes. Two armed Mexican men had been caught off guard. One of them stumbled and started to run. Mat leaped out, tackling the man, and they both fell to the ground. The other man stood motionless for a second, then dropped to his knees, letting his weapon drop to the ground.

One of the officers ran toward Mat and the Mexican and thrust his weapon into the Mexican's head, shouting, "Don't move a fucking muscle."

Mat stood and walked back toward Betty. He pulled out his phone and linked into a GPS system.

~ * ~

A man named Manny drove a black SUV down the dirt road. In the back of the vehicle sitting quietly was Juan Castro Lopez. The most powerful leader of one of the largest drug cartels operating in Mexico.

Manny looked into the rear-view mirror. "Sir, you sure you want to go to the tunnel?"

"I must inspect. I have heard there have been problems. We have very valuable cargo to deliver. There must not be problems." The driver shrugged and continued driving.

Mat had begun telling Betty about the positioning when they heard an approaching vehicle. The officers pulled the two handcuffed men back behind a clump of large bushes. Betty and Mat slid to the other side of the dirt road.

A black SUV pulled up and two men got out. They opened the hatchback and dragged out two large cases. The back door opened and a man in a black suit slid out of the car and gave out what sounded like commands to the two men.

Betty whispered, "He told them to take the cases into the tunnel." Matt didn't respond.

When the two men walked toward the tunnel, they noticed the door was open and the large clump of bushes was pulled aside. One of them called out something in Spanish.

"He is asking where the two guards are," Betty whispered.

The well-dressed man walked toward the opening. Mat caught the attention of one of the officers and gave him a signal to move out. The two officers jumped up and called out, "Everybody on the ground. Now!"

One of the men quickly turned and ran toward the SUV. The officers called out again. The other man dove behind a large tree and began running through the dense woods. Two officers chased after him.

The well-dressed man didn't move. The two officers with their weapons held high against their chests moved toward the man. Their helmets shone in the hot sun. Their chest protectors were firm and tight against their bodies. Again, they called out and announced who they were.

One of the men ran to the car, found his weapon, leaped out from the side and began to open fire. Both officers returned fire and the bullets smashed into the side of the car. They both hit the ground and continued to fire their weapons. The men yelled something is Spanish, threw his weapon in the air and raised his arms high toward the sky.

"Get down. Get down," the officer called out."

The man fell to the ground. He was quickly handcuffed and dragged away.

Mat had dived to the ground and Betty slid behind a thick brush. The man who gave the orders slid along the ground and picked up the dropped weapon. Mat called out, "Don't do it. Drop it."

The man grabbed the weapon and turned and scampered toward the car. Mat fired off a few rounds but missed him. The man ducked behind the car and waited a second, then turned and aimed his weapon and began to fire. Betty had moved in behind him. She moved slowly toward him. He didn't see her. She stretched out her arms and held her Glock with both hands, trying to keep from shaking. She was well trained and had been involved in several arrests but still she could feel her stomachache with anxiety. She stood a few feet from the man. She began to call out when he turned and saw her. He pulled up his weapon and started to aim it at her. She didn't hesitate and fired four rounds directly at him. All four bullets struck the man in the chest area. He fell back against the SUV, paused for a second then slid down the side of the car, leaving a trail of blood. His body slithered to the ground. Betty rushed over and kicked his weapon away.

Mat had seen it all. There was stillness in the air. It was over.

Mat walked over to Betty. "You okay?"

Betty stared down at the bloody man. "I don't know. It happened so fast. I had to react to what he did. He pointed his weapon at me and—"

Mat interrupted, "You did the right thing. You did really good."

Mat bent down and studied the man. He was dead. He looked closely at him. He recognized him. He looked at Betty. "You know who he is?"

"No."

"Well, you're about to be very, very famous. You just brought down the most dangerous and feared man in this part of Mexico. Juan Castro Lopez. The authorities have been after him for years. He is... or was, the leader of the largest and most violent cartel in Mexico. Congratulations."

Within an hour, the place was buzzing with the Mexican Federal Police, American border guards, officials from the DEA, FBI and Homeland Security. He and Betty were instructed to report to the office of Homeland Security to give a complete briefing.

Mat made a motion with his head and he Betty slipped through the bushes and into the tunnel. He grabbed her arm and said, "I looked into the cases. It wasn't weed. The cases were loaded with automatic weapons. You're about to be a star." A half hour later they exited the tunnel and drove off.

Twenty-four

They sat quietly, staring out the car window. Mat looked over. "Jesus, that's a first for me. All these years on the force and I've never been involved in a shootout like that."

"And you think I have. I was shaking all over the place."

"You didn't show it. From what I saw, you were very calm."

"I tried. I got this rush. All the training just came to me. I think I still have a rush."

"I do, too."

"My place or yours?" she asked.

Mat yanked the gear shift into D and the car roared down the street. They arrived at her apartment and raced inside. Betty ripped at her clothes and began stripping. Mat literally jumped on her and wrestled her to the floor. It didn't take long before they were both lost in a wild lustful embrace.

Betty hung on with both arms and her legs wrapped around Mat's body. His entire body gyrated as he reacted to her every move and emotion. The sweat poured from their bodies. It was as if they were stuck together. They both yelled out in ecstasy as they climaxed together.

Mat rolled over trying to catch his breath. He laughed out loud. "What the fuck was that? I got carpet burns on my knees and my body feels like it's been drenched in hot rain."

Betty laughed along with him. "I don't know what that was either, but I can tell you my butt is as raw as a rotten oyster."

"Unbelievable." Mat sighed.

Betty rolled over on top of him. She placed her lips close to his. "That, my friend, was some adrenaline rush. I've never felt emotion like that. Just the whole thing today. Us. Me and you taking charge. The SWAT team. The gunfire. The danger. Oh God, I loved it. And you were terrific. You were so much in control."

"And so were you."

She laid her head on his chest and he could feel her heart beating. After a few minutes, he could hear her soft sighs as she drifted off.

Mat closed his eyes and lowered his head. He wanted to shout out to her that he wasn't terrific. That he was a bad guy. A bad cop. A cop on the take. He was taking bribes from a drug lord. He was a criminal. He was withholding evidence. He had to hold back the tears as his emotions took control.

He reached over, pulled Betty up and carried her into her bedroom. He laid her gently on the bed, dressed and walked back into the kitchen. He searched for the tequila. He found the bottle and took a long swig. He walked out onto the small balcony and sat on a lounge chair. He drank from the bottle, taking one long swig after another. He had to get lost...lost in his world of lies, booze and self-destruction.

~ * ~

They stared at each other for a few minutes as they stood at the entrance to the security check point at the El Paso Airport. Betty stood next to him. He said, "I can't believe they make you go through security."

"Procedures are procedures."

"I know why you want to do this. It's called a body search. I know you love it when they pat you down."

Betty laughed. "I'll surprise them when I return the favor."

She was on her way back to Washington and a citation, followed by a promotion.

She had been recognized by the agency for her outstanding job in finding the tunnel and bringing down the leader of the cartel. Mat let her have all the publicity and rewards for what they had accomplished.

"So, I saw your interview on Fox News...you're famous."

"Just stop. I was asked to do it by my boss. And I am far from being famous."

"You're famous in Mexico. Your picture is all over the county."

"Just doing my job."

Mat grinned, "And a fine job it was."

It was true. Juan Castro Lopez was the most feared man in Mexico. It had been reported for years he didn't care if he killed men, women or children to get command of the drug trade and bringing in illegal immigrants into the U.S. After his death was reported, there was a rash of arrests that included not only the members of his cartel but politicians who had no one to protect them. For sure, Betty Vazquez was a national hero.

"Tell me, is CNN next?" Mat asked.

"I guess. I'm not too crazy about it, but the big boys tell me it will help bring attention to what the agency is accomplishing."

"You love it and you know it."

Betty smiled. "Maybe a little. But you know it should be about the both of us."

"We agreed that is something I do not want. It's your time to shine. Enjoy it."

Betty moved closer. She leaned up against him. "You know we could have had something here. Opposites do attract, you know."

Mat didn't have a response. Truth was he really did like her. But he knew nothing could ever come of their relationship. There would be no way he would move to Washington; even when she told him she could arrange a fat job for him.

The announcement called for the boarding of her plane. She picked up a small suitcase and started toward the line. She said, "I know I told you yesterday how much I learned from you. I do appreciate everything you did for me. You are a good guy. Sometime a little off center, but...oh well, I'll miss you."

Mat didn't respond.

She leaned over and gave him a kiss on the lips. She whispered, "And a good lay, too."

Twenty-five

Mat found his way to The Pink Lady. He was to meet Bones, the man who replaced Jamar. For a few minutes, Mat dropped back into his feeling guilty mode. It seemed to go away after his third shot of tequila.

Sometimes it didn't help. He had been feeling guiltier and guiltier every day. Ever since Betty left, he had been drowning himself in self-pity. He had to face the fact that he missed her. He hadn't been assigned a new partner and wasn't in any hurry to have one.

After they found the tunnel the pressure was taken off him. His boss gave him a citation and he was recognized by the police commissioner. All the time he was breaking the law. He was a crooked cop, a drunk and one of the bad guys. He decided to make a change. Tonight was the last money he would take from Fat Baby. He had decided to ask Sue to move in with him and have a normal life; as normal as a police officer could have.

He spotted her and watched as she did her dance on the stage. Her nude body shone in the array of colored lights that flashed across her. The loud music pounded through his head and the lights left him dizzy. He staggered to the round stage and threw a ten dollar on the stage. She slithered over, grabbed the money, kissed him on the check and rolled across the stage.

Mat had yet to meet his new contact. He had a description. It didn't take him long to spot him. He was tall, at least six four, with short black hair. He was thin but well proportioned. Mat walked closer and noticed his features. He was black, but his skin was light and smooth. He was surrounded by three dancers.

Mat stood next to him. He kept his eyes on the stage. He said softly, "You Bones?"

"That'd be me. You must be Mat."

"Let's keep this simple. Just lower your hand straight down below the bar and hand it to me."

Bones reached into his back pocket and pulled out a small white envelope. He did what Mat suggested and let his arm fall straight down. Mat turned around and with one motion grabbed the envelope out of his hand. He said, "Every Tuesday, same place, but two hours later. Work for you?"

"Whatever."

Mat slid the envelope in his pocket. He turned toward Bones. "Ready for a drink?"

"Sure. Bourbon on the rocks."

Mat ordered the drinks. "I hear Jamar is out of town."

"You could say that," Bones replied. He took a drink. "You seem to be well known around here."

"Been hanging around for a while. See the dancer on the stage. Taken."

"Nice. There are a few hot ladies in here. I think I'll like coming here more often."

Mat downed his shot. He said, "Be cool, Bones. I'll see you next Tuesday."

The next Tuesday seemed to come too fast for Mat. He was still trying to find a way to cut the cord with Fat Baby. He entered The Pink Lady and spotted Bones. He was going to refuse the money and tell him to tell Fat Baby the deal was over. He started toward him when Bones saw him and came up to him. "Come on. I want to show you something."

"What? Now?"

"Yeah. Let's go."

Mat followed Bones out of the club and into his car. Bones drove through town, found the interstate and drove west about five miles. He exited and made a few turns and slowed down on a dark street lined with older houses. He pulled over and turned off the engine.

"These three houses on this side of the street and two on the other side are part of Fat Baby's meth houses."

"How nice. Now why are you showing me this shit?"

"See the van parked over there?" Bones pointed a block up the street.

"Hardly. The street is so dark. Jesus."

"That van is ours."

"Ours?"

"Yes. It belongs to Fat Baby. You were on the team the last time I looked."

"Why bring me here?"

Bones reached into the glove compartment. He pulled out an envelope. "Here."

Mat grabbed the envelope and began to put it into his pocket.

Bones touched his arm. "Open it."

"Why"

"Just open it."

Mat shrugged his shoulders and ripped open the end. He pulled out the money. He counted five thousand, five hundred dollars. He looked over at Bones. "What the hell is this?"

"Fat Baby wanted to let you know he expects you to drive around the street a few times at night. Check it out. Make sure we don't have a repeat of the last attack."

"Not going to happen. I'll take my five hundred and you can give him back the rest. As a matter of fact, give it all back to him. Our deal is over."

"I wouldn't do that if I were you. You're in. Get it. Don't be fucking with him. You made the deal, remember. You just can't say no and walk away. He may not go for it and I wouldn't begin to think what he is capable of doing. Plus, five grand extra is a nice piece of change."

Mat felt an empty feeling deep in the pit of his stomach. He knew Bones was right. He was in too deep. He had made the deal. "And what the hell does he expect me to do if I see something?"

"Hey, you're the cop. Arrest somebody. Call for backup. Hell, I don't know."

"And the van?"

"They're here for a pickup. If they saw something they'd probably help. But the man wants you here. What can I say? Plus, this is the only house left. He closed the other houses down. Don't know why, but he did."

Mat sat quietly in his seat. Bones looked over and said, "You know, I don't get this. I read about you. You're big news. Big time arrest record. And here you are taking money from a drug dealer. What's the story with that?"

"I don't want to talk about it. It's none of your fucking business."

"Just asking, that's all."

"Well, don't. I'll do this, but you can tell him this. If I see something that looks like an attack, I'll contact you and you call for backup. I've told him many times I can't get involved in his drug business. Not my job. I make one arrest, and believe me, the boys in the DE group will know what I'm doing in a heartbeat."

Bones started the car and drove down the dark street. Mat put the money in his pocket. "Take me to a bar. I need to get drunk."

"I got some good ice."

"Fuck off."

Bones dropped Mat at The Pink Lady. He didn't feel like going back inside. He found his car and drove directly to the bar on the border. He couldn't believe how deep he was in with Fat Baby. He knew he couldn't walk away. He had known a few cops who were arrested for taking bribes and several others for stealing drugs for resale.

He began to feel guilty. He felt the pain inside for thinking he could take bribes and keep information from his fellow officers. The only way he could live with himself was to drown his mind with tequila. He drank himself drunk.

Mat staggered from the bar and found his car. He fumbled with his keys and finally started the engine. He roared out of the parking lot and drove hard through the dark street. He flew through a red light and pressed the gas petal hard to the floor. The top was down, and the warm wind blasted against his face. He didn't see the flashing blue lights but heard the siren.

He looked into the rear-view mirror and saw the black and white as it grew closer. He slowed down, pulled over and waited.

The police officer approached the car and walked around to the passenger side. He stood erect and glared at Mat and commanded, "Driver's license and registration, please."

Mat pulled his detective badge from his waist and pushed it toward the police officer. The officer grabbed the badge and studied it. He dropped it on the seat. "I don't know what the hell you're doing...and I don't care if you kill yourself. I just don't want you killing a civilian."

Mat didn't respond.

"You smell like a bottle of tequila. You're drunk. Very drunk. I suggest you pull into the parking area over there and I'll drive you home."

Mat stuttered, "Call me a cab."

The officer made a call. "I'll be waiting in my car until the cab comes. And do something foolish like racing away, detective or not, I'll bring you down." He turned, walked away and whispered, "Asshole."

Mat lowered his head. He was sinking lower and he knew it. He just didn't know how to get out of the mess he'd gotten himself into.

Twenty-six

Hector was not a happy man. He was very nervous as he drove his pickup to a house in Juarez. It was the first time in two years he was going to meet with one of the drug people. Since the first meeting, he never had to meet anybody in person. The chemicals were always put into his truck on Monday evening along with an envelope with his payoff.

He located the house, parked the truck and walked up the steps. The door opened, and a man wave at him. He walked in and found it dark but well kept. The man spoke, "Hector, welcome. Come in and sit."

He groped his way to a large leather chair and sat. The man continued, "You have served us well for many years. You have proven to be a very good solider. But things have changed. We have one more run for you and then we will not need your services."

Hector began to feel the sweat stream down his face. He became more nervous. He stuttered, "I don't understand. If I have done well why am I being replaced?"

"There are new people in charge now and they have different ways to supply the chemicals."

"I don't understand. I…"

"You don't have to. Just listen to what I will say to you. Tomorrow you will arrive here at six a.m. A body suit will be strapped under your clothes and there will be two million dollars in it. You will be instructed where to deliver the money. When you return, I will pay you ten thousand dollars. You then can go home and enjoy the money. Now, leave and be here tomorrow morning."

"But..."

"There are no buts. You have been chosen to deliver this money because you are trustworthy and dependable. You will do nothing different than you do every Tuesday morning. You will act the same. Instead of going to the café and dropping off the case, you will have an address and a GPS. When you arrive, go inside, strip off your clothes and leave the body suit. You then can go to work as usual."

"I...It..."

"Now, there is no more to say. Please. Leave."

Hector drove to his favorite café. He ordered a bottle of tequila and sat outside. He was trying to figure what had just happened to him. He tried to imagine some kind of body suit that would fit under his clothes and could hold two million dollars. His whole body shook as he drank shot after shot.

~ * ~

Mat reached for his ringing cell phone. It was Fat Baby. "What's up?"

"Memorize this address. One-one-six-four-six El Camino Real. Be there next Tuesday at nine a.m. and pick up a large suitcase. When you have the case, call me and I will tell you where to deliver it."

Mat cut him off. "Hey, this is going way beyond what I signed up for. I am not your errand boy."

"For fifty large, you will be my errand boy...now won't you?"

"Whoa...that's a big number. I don't want to sound ungrateful, but Fat Baby, I will not whip around the city with drugs in my car."

"Trust is an overused word. I use it myself a lot because I am trustworthy and know when I can trust people. You will not be picking up drugs. I would never ask you to do that."

"Can I ask what the hell I will be picking up then?"

"You don't have to ask. You know."

Mat didn't hesitate. "Money. Lots of it."

"Remember trust. I chose you because I know I can trust you to do this. And by paying you more than I would pay anybody else, I know I am getting the best man for the job."

"How about this then...last time. Our relationship is over after this."

"You'll never hear my voice after you deliver the money. And I will never hear yours." There was dead silence.

Mat did what he always did when he needed time to think. He drove to the race-track in New Mexico. He seemed to think better around a noisy crowd.

He sat in the corner watching the several screens showing tracks around the country. Off track betting. He loved it. He finished several beers and bet on a harness race somewhere in the north, night horse racing from Louisiana and dog racing from Florida. He didn't care if he won or lost. He had to have the action.

He couldn't help thinking he was about to make a major mistake by picking up the money for Fat Baby. It was too easy. He still was a cop, and this was as wrong as anything could be. He thought it could be a setup. What an easy way to end my relationship with the new drug cartel. He began to imagine all type of scenarios. He could see the entire police force waiting for him. He could see the new drug cartel ending his life on the spot. He could be walking into a trap.

Mat walked around the betting area. He found his way to one of the many bars. His mind was racing. Then it hit him. He would send Sue to pick up the money. He would be waiting at her place. When she returned with the money, he would take it to Fat Baby, collect fifty big ones and then grab Sue and head out of town. He could see them hiding out for a while. Maybe in Mexico. On the coast. He had been to La Paz once. He loved it. The money could go a long way down there. A coolness came over him as he walked out into the humid night.

Twenty-seven

Fred Cummings slept late. He didn't even hear his wife as she dressed and left for work. He had returned from a trip to Fort Hood, an Army base located in central Texas. He had attended a meeting to review a contract his company had recently been awarded to do all the electrical work as part of a large award to a prime contractor.

The meeting lasted two days and consisted of the representatives from the base, the contracting person from the Army, who made the award and the contractor who had won with the best proposal. Fred's part of the meeting was to do an overview of the financial aspects of his company's portion of the contract as the sub-contractor to do the electrical work. The company's team of electrical engineers did most of the presentation. He had to sit through one boring presentation after another to present his part, less than twenty minutes.

He awoke after nine, grabbed his cell phone, poured a cold glass of orange juice and went out to the patio. He sat, punched in a few numbers and called his boss.

"Morning Russell, I wanted to give you a call with an update. The plane was delayed, and I didn't get in till after midnight. I'll be working at home for few hours."

Russell replied, "Go on."

During the past year, Fred had worked with the sales team and they had produced winning proposals for several large government contracts. Fred was to receive several large cash bonuses and a plaque from the CEO of the company. He noticed his immediate boss seemed to act cold toward him, at times not returning phone calls or answering his e-mails. Fred began to believe his boss feared he would soon be fired, and he would replace him.

Fred continued, "The meeting went very well and as a matter of fact we were able to secure another fifty thousand dollars for several change orders. The contract was amended on the spot."

"Okay," Russell answered.

Fred shook his head. He couldn't believe how distant and disinterested Russell sounded. "We should be able to start work within a month."

There were a few minutes of an uneasy silence. Fred waited for a response. Finally, he said, "I'm going to be working at home in the mornings for the next few days. A new bid came out from the county and I want to break it down from a financial standpoint before I meet with the sales team."

"Whatever." Russell hung up.

Fred almost threw his cell phone across the room. He couldn't believe how his boss had been acting lately, and now this. He had worked for months with the sales team on the proposal, making sure the quote was accurate and the profit was sufficient. When the final numbers were added to the proposal, he had felt confident the price quote was competitive and the company would have a chance to win. They had been awarded the contract and it was one of the largest awards the company had ever won.

Fred called his wife. "I just talked to Russell. He acted like a jerk."

"He's afraid you're going to get his job. Come on, we both know he's useless. He's looking over his shoulder and you're the threat he's seeing."

"I guess. But you'd think he'd be excited about the award."

"Let me put it this way. You're going to get a big bonus...he won't. Get it?"

Fred had to laugh. "I got it all right. What do you think I should do?"

"Nothing. Lie in the weeds, head down, do your job and good things will happen."

"Agreed. Celebrate tonight?"

"Let's do it."

"I'm going to work at home for a while and go in around two for a couple of hours."

"I'll be home at seven and we'll go out to dinner."

"Love you."

"Love you, too."

~ * ~

Two days later Fred was working at home. His cell phone rang with a call from his boss. "Hello, Russell. What's up?"

"I want to make this as short and painless as I can. As of today, you are on paid suspension from the company."

Fred was stunned. He hesitated, trying to collect his thoughts. Russell continued, "You need to be here tomorrow at eight in the morning to meet with Canterbury. You are to stop working on any projects and have no contact with anybody, representing yourself as an employee of..."

Fred shouted, "What the fuck are you talking about? What's going on, Russell?"

"It is what I said. Be here tomorrow. Be on time." The phone went dead.

Fred stood and walked around his home office in a daze. His mind was muddled and confused. He couldn't think. He had to call somebody. He thought of Marcia Jennings, Director of Human Resources. He quickly dialed her number.

"I just got a call from Russell. He said I am on paid suspension. What the hell does that mean?"

"Fred, I am not at liberty to discuss this with you now. I am sure he told you to be here tomorrow morning at eight and..."

Fred interrupted, "I know what he said. I believe I have a right to know why."

"You will be briefed tomorrow. That is all I can say."

He shouted, "You expect me to go the rest of the day and tonight not knowing what the hell is going on? Huh?"

"Just do as Russell said. And remember to bring your laptop with you and all your files. Bye, Fred."

Fred sat quietly staring at the wall. His mind was racing. He said aloud, "It's Russell. That bastard. He did something to make this happen."

He thought, *I can't tell Janice until I know what has happened. How could this happen. I've done nothing to deserve this kind of action.* He kept mumbling to himself. *They want my files. My laptop. I will be let go. Why?*

Fred left the house and began driving. He didn't know where he was going...he had to get out of the house. He was confused, devastated and scared to death.

Twenty-eight

Fred arrived before eight and walked directly toward Richard Canterbury's office. Richard was president of the company. After Fred had been hired he found out Strategic Electronic was a division of a nationwide conglomerate. He learned Richard had profit and loss responsibility for his division and watched every penny the company spent. When Fred took the job, he thought he was working for a privately-owned electrical contractor. As it turned out it didn't matter to him. He had proven himself and was able to bring the financial knowledge that helped the company grow revenue very quickly.

Nobody was around as he stood in front of the door. Before he could knock, the door opened. Richard called out, "Come in, Fred. Sit down."

Fred sat in a leather chair directly in front of Richard's desk. He looked over and saw Marcia Jennings sitting to his left. He waited for Richard to walk around and sit at his chair behind his desk. For a few minutes, nobody said a word. Fred was waiting for Richard to start. He noticed his boss, Russell, was not present.

"Fred, this isn't easy. But I am afraid we have decided you are to be let go today." He raised his hand. "Now, before you react. I want to tell you this is a very serious matter and we needed to act quickly. You are being let go because it came to our attention that you manipulated the numbers on several of the pricing pages, we submitted for several contracts we won so you could receive the bonus money. You have committed a serious offense against the code of conduct as outlined in the offer letter you signed."

Fred was stunned. His mind was having trouble comprehending what he had heard. He shook his head and finally said, "You've got to be kidding. I don't even know what the hell you're talking about. You're saying I did something to the price quotes. I did the pricing, but the pricing was reviewed by...wait, by you and..."

"Fred, stop. After going back and reviewing the numbers, you bid a very low price and have put this company in a very serious cash flow problem. By winning the last two contracts, the company could lose millions."

Fred jumped up and shouted, "That's bullshit, and you know it. I worked those numbers and I know the margins. We made over twenty percent on both deals. We're talking millions in revenue at a healthy profit. This contract was the company's biggest win and with the best margin. We stand to make millions in profit."

"No. That's what you wanted us to believe. The truth is, you worked the numbers so low and left out much of the work that had to be done so we would win, and you would get those bonuses we talked about. By leaving out hundreds of thousands of dollars in work we are committed to do, you have, well, hurt the finances of this company. We will have to complete the work and not be paid by the government for doing it."

Fred turned to Marcia. "What is going on here? I have my rights. I have the numbers right here. I want to go over each one line by line. You'll see that every requirement was priced. Nothing was left out."

Marcia did not respond. He turned back to Canterbury. "Come on. Let's go over these price sheets. I have them right here on my computer." Fred began to reach for his briefcase."

"Don't, Fred, it's too late. It's been decided. Marcia has a check for you which covers the rest of the week and..."

Fred's mind went blank. He didn't hear the rest of what Canterbury was saying. He sat motionless. His body seemed to collapse.

Marcia said, "Leave your laptop on the desk and empty your briefcase. Someone from security will escort you to your desk. Please take your personal items only."

Fred stood and lowered his head. He took a deep breath and tried to collect his thoughts. He started to turn toward the door. A thought raced through his mind. He figured it out.

He looked at Canterbury. "I get it. It's the bonus money. I reviewed my offer letter last night. It stated I would receive seven percent of all contracts we won that I worked the financial numbers on. I figured, based on the two wins, I would receive over two hundred and seventy thousand dollars. You don't want to pay me. It would fuck up your expenses." He laughed. "And you wouldn't get *your* profit bonus. You never figured we would win these big contracts. Well, we did. I did. I did it with my unique pricing format and competitive numbers. And when you sat down with upper management you realized I would receive over a quarter of a million dollars. You didn't figure that in the expense ratio. It would screw the numbers for the quarter, and *you'd* be out *your* bonus and I would get mine."

Canterbury walked toward the door and opened it. He said, "You're no longer an employee of this company. Clear out your desk and get out."

Fred walked half way through the door, turned and said, "See you in court, you selfish bastard."

~ * ~

Fred drove around the desert for hours. He wasn't sure how to tell his wife. He found a small café and drank several tequila shots and left for home. He found Janice in the kitchen. She said, "You're very late. You didn't call."

"I was...was...I need a drink."

He walked past Janice to one of the cabinets. She said, "You smell like a bottle of tequila. You all right?"

"Just fucking great."

"Fred, you're drunk. I've never seen you like this. What is going on?"

He stopped and turned toward her. "I'll tell you what's going on. I was let go. Fired. Hear me?" he shouted, "Fired!"

Janice was stunned. "Fired? What the hell happened?"

Fred poured tequila into a shot glass and gulped it down. He poured another. Janice stepped forward and put her hand over the glass. "Enough. Tell me what happened."

Fred staggered backward. He felt the counter with his hands and said, "Canterbury said I fudged the numbers so we would win so I would be paid the bonuses."

"I... I don't understand."

Fred found his way to a chair and sat. "It's a game. A joke. He said I left out work that had to be completed and put the company at risk. The truth is he doesn't want to pay me my bonuses. If he does, he won't receive his bonuses. Get it? He fucked me, so he could make his profit number and get paid off. By paying me it would exceed his expenses to profit ratio. I know all this. I do the paperwork. That rat bastard."

Janice stood silent. She moved slowly around the kitchen and sat in front of Fred. She asked, "What the hell are we going to do?"

"Find a good attorney and sue the bastards."

"I mean about money. About this house. You know I do okay, but the flower shop doesn't make enough to pay for all this."

Fred jumped up from the table, knocking the chair to the floor. "Damn it, Janice, I'll find something. We have enough money in our money market account to last a few months."

"Great. A few months. So how much severance pay did you get?"

Fred lowered his head. "None. He said I was let go due to a moral clause and non- compliance with company policy."

"Jesus, Fred, what the hell are we going to do?"

Twenty-nine

Hector Morales had never been so nervous in his entire life. He arrived at the house at six in the morning. He parked his car, shut off the engine, and sat quietly thinking about what he was about to do. Nothing seemed right. He knew he would be paid a lot of money and when he drove across the border it wouldn't be any different than the thousands of times he'd done it. But still something was making him sick to his stomach.

He slipped out of the car and walked toward the front door. As he reached for the doorknob, the door flew open. Inside, a man called out, "Right on time, my friend."

Hector didn't reply. The man continued, "I have the money suit already to go. Please disrobe. This is a very good piece. It will be taped to your body. The money is in there."

Hector took off his shirt and pants. He looked at the money suit. It was white with little pockets. The material felt like silk. It was thin and long.

The man began to wrap the suit around Hector's body. He took a roll of tape and began to twist the tape starting right below his armpits and wrapped it all the way to Hector's legs.

"How does that feel?"

"It's okay. It is light."

The man laughed, "Not bad for holding two million dollars."

Hector pulled up his pants and put on his shirt. It felt tight but wasn't noticeable.

The man stepped back. "There. Nothing looks out of place. Just do what you do. I know your routine. You will go through the border crossing as usual. Drive to the house and deliver. You have a cell phone?"

"Yes. Why?"

"Give it to me. I don't want you to call anyone, or for you to get a call."

"But..."

"Just give me the phone."

Hector handed him his cell phone. The man said, "Here is a GPS and a slip of paper with the address. You know how to use one of these?"

"Yes. We use them at the nursery."

"Good. When you leave here, plug in the address and you'll find the house. Walk in, disrobe, and do it quickly. Return here for your payoff."

Hector turned and walked out to his car. He was walking stiffly, but he didn't care. He didn't worry. He had never had to get out of his car in the past.

He approached the border. The line of cars seemed longer. He slowed down. He looked at his clock on the dashboard. He was early. He became very nervous. His mind was running wild. He was out of his routine. The border guards would be a different crew. They wouldn't know him. They might ask him to get out of the truck. The dogs would sniff him. He couldn't think. He decided to turn around. Go back home and wait. He tried to turn the car around. The lines on both sides were too long. A blast of a horn from the car behind him startled him. He looked ahead. He hadn't noticed the car in front had moved up. He had no choice.

He was next. The car in front moved away. He inched up to the guard at his station. He didn't recognize the guard. His hand shook as he reached for his work visa. He handed it to the guard. The man looked at the visa and back at Hector. He could feel the sweat forming on his neck. He tried a fake smile. It was taking too long. He tried to remain calm. Something wasn't right.

"Hector. I see you're going in early this morning."

Hector relaxed. He didn't recognize the guard, but he seemed to know him. He stuttered, "Yes...yes...I..."

"Have a good one." He handed the visa back to Hector.

Hector breathed a sigh of relief as he drove down the road. He was through. Step one was completed.

Thirty

A man known only as Charlie sat in a comfortable lounge chair in his dark living room. He had been there since five in the morning. He had been informed by Fat Baby he would be the recipient of two million dollars. He would count the money, take twenty thousand for himself and wait for a man by the name of Mat to pick it up.

Charlie had been Fat Baby's accountant for many years, even before Fat Baby worked his way into the drug business. He was paid well for his services. Enough for him to live in a nice house, drive a luxury car and make a few trips to Vegas each year.

This was the first time he had ever done this type of transaction. He knew Fat Baby was a gangster. A bad guy. But all he did was keep a set of books for him and do his taxes each year. On occasion, he would help Fat Baby launder money. Another transaction he knew was illegal. And it didn't hurt that he had the best connection to supply his meth habit.

Charlie knew what he did was against the law. But he had consulted an attorney who was also represented Fat Baby. The lawyer assured him he was just an accountant who didn't know what kind of work his client did. He just was paid to do his taxes and other accounting jobs.

He prepared a good dose of meth, sat back and closed his eyes waiting for the person who was to pick up the money. He fingered his plane ticket to Vegas. He would leave for the airport as soon as the money was picked up. He didn't really understand why Fat Baby was going through such an elaborate plan to receive money coming out of Juarez. All he knew was to receive the money, take his share, and someone would pick up the remainder.

Charlie began to wonder as he waited for the delivery of the money. He often thought back to his days in college at North Texas State. It was then he had become friends with several football players. He had a good reason. He tutored several team members in math. One of the players was a large black man by the name of Eugene Thompson.

Eugene always said if it weren't for Charlie, he would never have been able to keep his scholarship and continue on the football team. Charlie used to say if it weren't for Eugene he wouldn't have had the social life he'd had in college.

Charlie was quiet, studious and shy. He wasn't very popular in high school and didn't change much when he went to North Texas State. He was just another student who went unrecognized around the campus. But Charlie was good at one thing: math. He excelled both in high school and college. When he was approached by the athletic department to tutor several football and basketball players, he agreed when he found out he would be paid for his time.

During his senior year, he developed a relationship with Eugene. After they graduated, Charlie kept in touch with him and learned Eugene had moved to El Paso. At that time, Eugene was working for an oil company in its marketing department. Charlie was working as an accountant in a small firm. They connected, and Charlie did his taxes. Charlie smiled to himself when he recalled a phone conversation, he'd had two years earlier.

~ * ~

"Charlie. It's Eugene. How you doin'?"

"Hey, Eugene, what is going on? We haven't talked in almost a year. I tried calling the number you gave me, but it was disconnected."

"I've been movin' around, you know. You still with that firm?"

"Still here and hating every minute of it. But it's a paycheck. What can I say?"

"Well, you're about to get promoted."

"How's that?"

"First, my name is now Fat Baby..."

Charlie cut him off. "What? What the hell is...did you say Fat Baby?"

"Just listen for a minute. I am no longer Eugene Thompson. Get it. From now on call me Fat Baby. And I'm hiring you to do the books for my company."

"Okay. I guess. I mean..."

"How much are you making at that company?"

"Forty thousand a year."

"How's one hundred thou sound?"

"Pardon?"

"I never will forget how you taught me how to really use computers. I mean really use them. And the way you trained me on working a spreadsheet. Without your help and training I wouldn't have been able to accomplish what I have today."

"Thanks Eugene tha..."

Fat Baby snapped, "It's Fat Baby. Don't forget that. I need you to meet me at the Main Street Café around noon tomorrow. I will fill you in...and welcome aboard." The phone went dead before Charlie could respond.

Now two years later, Charlie Longstreet still couldn't believe Fat Baby was a drug lord and he was living a great life at 11646 El Camino Real; a quiet street in El Paso.

~ * ~

Mat made the call. Fat Baby answered. "Change of plans. I'm sending a lady to pick up the money."

There was a long silence on the other end. Finally, Fat Baby said, "I don't like this. I told you why I chose you. Remember; trust. Why this change?"

"You should know I wouldn't do this unless it was the best way. I'm being cautious. If your plan has a flaw and the authorities are alerted, I stand a chance of being the one who gets caught. I can't take that chance."

"Then who?"

"Just a lady friend. She is in this with me."

Mat could easily detect a change in Fat Baby's voice. "Let me say this, my friend. If you fuck this up, I can guarantee you will not live long enough to remember your own name."

"I won't let it happen." The phone went dead.

Mat joined Sue in the bedroom. She was sitting on the bed.

"You going to tell me what I am picking up."

"You don't need to know."

"Oh, that's cool. I get to where I'm going and the person hands me a bag of shit and I say, oh, thanks. Come on, I need to know so I can make sure I'm not getting screwed."

"You won't get screwed. The person knows what he has to do."

"Drugs. Its drugs, ain't it? I don't like that. I may smoke a joint with you, but I don't like..."

"It's not drugs. It's a business deal. That's all you need to know."

Sue reached over and grabbed the snub nosed .38 pistol Mat had given her. She laughed and pointed it at Mat. He screamed, "Jesus, how many times have I told you not to do that."

"There's no bullets in it," Sue said.

"I don't give a damn. Put it down."

"I like it. And I did damn good with it at the range. I hit the target every time." She pointed the gun toward the ceiling. "Bang. Bang...got you."

"Come on, Sue, this is not funny. You may have to use it. Who knows?"

"I'll be ready...bang...bang."

~ * ~

Charlie answered his cell. "Hello."

120

"A change in plans. A lady will be picking up the money. It's seven. The delivery should be on time. Eight. The pickup is at nine. Do your thing and have it in a suitcase."

"Got it, man."

"And remember...trust."

"Yeah...yeah...trust." He heard a buzzing sound in his ear.

~ * ~

It hadn't been a good couple of weeks for Fred. He met with a lawyer and gave him a copy of all his documents relating to the two contracts the company had received. Two days later, the attorney called and said after reviewing all the information it appeared to be very complicated and it would take his staff at least two months to understand how to prepare the briefs and be able to file a suit. Fred felt like he didn't seem too enthused on taking the case.

He had also been networking. He had been disappointed at the fact several companies he had worked with showed no interest when he talked to them. He had a great story to tell. He had been with Strategic Electronics for two years. It was well documented he was personally responsible in taking a small, local electronic sub-contractor who worked mainly small jobs and growing them into a well-known company, winning large contracts not only with the local government but with the federal government as well. He had tripled their revenue in two years.

None of that seemed to matter. He could only think Canterbury had put out some bad and false information about him. He was desperately trying to find out if it was true. He could use this type of slander in his lawsuit.

He spent part of the day reviewing their financial position. With the money Janice was bringing in from the flower shop and the unemployment plus the money in their money market account, he figured they could last about six months. After that there wouldn't be enough cash left or coming in to pay their bills. His only thought was if he couldn't land a similar position with similar pay he would have to put a second mortgage on the house. Something Janice was absolutely against. He had to tell himself to stay calm and work harder to find a job.

Fred sat in his office in a white tee-shirt and a pair of boxer shorts. He hadn't shaved or showered in two days. He had hardly seen Janice in several days. She would leave very early in the morning before he woke and wouldn't return until after nine each night. She was working the extra hours hoping to bring in more revenue.

Fred was surviving on soup and sandwiches. He spent hours every day on the computer and on the phone. At first, he was confident he would land a job quickly but as it turned out, he was a statistic, an unemployed executive. He had been ashamed to file for unemployment but when he heard the amount, he would receive he filed online and was about to receive his first check.

"Fuck 'em," he called out. "I'll find a job with the competition and bury that bastard."

Thirty-one

The Captain watched intently as the news of Juan Carlos's death was reported. He too had feared the man. He had tried for years to meet him and form a large and powerful cartel. But he was untouchable. He wanted it all. There were some people who told The Captain it was his men who killed the professor so the blame would fall on him and Juan could take over his operation.

He picked up his phone.

"I have been told by several people it is time for me to return to Mexico and take charge. I am not ready. My family is in Spain and I just returned from visiting them. They are happy there. And if everything I have planned takes place, I will be able to join them and live a very comfortable life."

The voice on the other end replied, "You are a weak man. You have let people take your strength away from you. Your time is now. There is no leader. The country cries for you. Mexico is a poor country. It is drug exporting that fuels our economy. You know all the right people in our government who will work with us. They know what we do benefits our country."

The man known as The Captain remained silent. The other man continued to talk. "I am arranging a meeting in Mexico City. I know some people to invite. I need you and your list to complete the meeting. Our time is now."

"I am sorry. I will not attend." The buzzing sound echoed in his ear as the conversation ended.

The Captain knew the members of his team involved in the transaction to bring the two million dollars into the States were nervous. It wasn't the amount that kept him on edge. It was the people involved with carrying it out that worried him. To some of the people, two million big ones was a life changing amount. To the drug dealers it was a few weeks of dealings.

The new members of cartel were very concerned. Everybody involved was part of Fat Baby's team. At any time, someone along the way could be tempted to take the money and run.

The Captain had been informed from an inside man in Fat Baby's operation that an El Paso detective was to pick up the money. His name was Mat. He did make some calls and was able to learn the address of the house to which the money was to be delivered.

He sat at a long table with his men. "We have done well. But it is time to begin to take control of the fat man's operation. We must watch this transaction that is going to take place this morning. We have found out through an inside source the address of the delivery. A two-man team is on their way as we speak. If anything goes wrong, it will be our chance to make a move."

One of the men spoke. "What if we make it go wrong? What if the deal does not go down as planned? We then tell the fat man his team can no longer be trusted, and we are taking over the operation."

The Captain sat silent. He was interested in what his associate had said. He looked over at him. "What are your thoughts?"

"We must remember this is our money. We are giving it to Fat Baby for a show of good faith. If the money does not make it to his hands, there will be accusations. We will accuse him of having untrustworthy people on his team. He will accuse us of taking the money back. We will tell him we knew nothing about how the money was to be delivered. All we did was drop off the money at the house of one of his people in Juarez. Either way he is caught in the middle.

It will be our chance to take control of a weakened man. He will then work for us...completely."

"So, you suggest we intercept the money. Blame it on his men. He should kill all of them because he will not know who is telling the truth or who is lying. He could never suspect us. We will have our money back and then take control."

Another man spoke. "This must be done correctly. We have very little time to decide. The money is on its way. We can do this if we act quickly."

"I am concerned about one thing. The man who is picking up the money is a detective. We must be careful. I can only think this man is on Fat Baby's payroll, but I still want to be cautious. I like the plan, but we need to make sure it goes down the way Fat Baby planned it. I believe it will be best if we have two of our men follow the detective and inform us when the pickup is made. We do know the money will then be delivered to the fat man. At that point, we will make our move and take control before the money is delivered. I will be in contact with our people and instruct them to observe and follow. We will then have time to make our move."

~ * ~

Fred grabbed a cup of coffee and gazed out toward the back yard. An evening rain had cooled down the temperature. He pulled the large sliding glass doors open as wide as they could go. He took a deep breath and stood enjoying the cool breeze.

Janice had already left for her day at the flower shop. She had been leaving earlier every morning. Several mornings Fred would still be sleeping when she left the house.

Their relationship seemed to be deteriorating over the past weeks. Janice had become cold and distant. She constantly worried about money and was dead set against a second mortgage. Fred knew the numbers and it was the only way they could keep the house.

Fred slumped down in the lounge chair and took a long swig of coffee. He was surprised and disappointed that the several companies he felt sure would offer him a job had not responded to his e-mails or phone messages. Again, he thought for sure his old bosses were spreading stories about him. He had to do something about it. He had to confront Russell and Canterbury.

He finished his coffee and walked back into the living room. He talked out loud, "I'll turn off the air conditioner. The morning breeze is cool enough." It seemed Fred had been talking out loud to himself more and more each day.

~ * ~

Hector wasn't himself as he drove through the maze of streets. He was listening to the voice on the GPS giving him instructions. He continued to look into both of his mirrors as he drove slowly down the quiet streets. He felt for sure he was being followed. He knew they were on to him. He couldn't control his mind. He wanted it to end.

He continued to listen to the female voice on the GPS. He made a left turn and found the street. Earlier he had punched in the house number; 11464 El Camino Real. He stretched to see the numbers on the mailboxes in front of the houses. The voice said, 'You have arrived."

Hector turned off the engine and sat motionless. He closed his eyes, took a deep breath and bolted from the car. He walked quickly up the long cement walkway. He pounded on the door. His whole body shook as he waited for someone to open it. It seemed to take forever. He pounded again. He kept looking back, to the left, to the right. His head was on a spindle.

Finally, the door opened. Hector stared at a man standing in front of him in a white tee-shirt and boxer trunks. He didn't hesitate. He pushed open the door and stormed into the house. Fred called out, "What the hell? Hey, you..."

Hector shouted, "I want this to be over." He ripped off his shirt and pulled down his pants and began ripping the tape off his body.

Fred stood there in amazement. He moved closer to Hector. "What's going on? Who are you? Why are you...what the hell are you doing?"

Hector didn't reply as he pulled the last piece of tape away from his legs and threw the white suit to the floor. "It is over. It is yours now. Sign this and I will be going."

Fred reached down and picked up the suit. He could see through several pockets and saw it was money. It didn't take him long to figure it was a lot of money.

"What is this? Who are you? You can't just bust into my house and…"

Hector shoved a piece of paper in Fred's face. "Please, sign. I want to go."

Again, Fred ran his fingers along the suit. He pulled aside one of the pockets and thumbed the cash.

Hector yelled, "Come on, man. Sign the paper."

For a few minutes, Fred was lost in space. His mind went blank. He turned and ran to his office and came back with a pen. He grabbed the piece of paper and scribbled a series of unrecognizable letters. He handed it back to Hector. The Mexican grabbed the paper and ran toward the door and to his truck. Before Fred could even react, the truck roared down the street.

Confused and dazed, Fred pulled the white suit into his office. He started to rip open the pockets. He saw dollar bills. Some were five hundred dollar bills. Some were one thousand dollar bills. He began ripping open the rest of the pockets at a fierce pace. The money was flying all over his office.

Fred finished counting. He said softly, "Two fucking million dollars."

He sat staring at the money. Every possible scenario ran through his mind. It had to be bad money. It was for sure delivered to the wrong address. The Mexican had made a mistake. He had to call the police. He had to report this. But what would they say? He would be questioned for hours. They would come to his house. The neighbors would see them. They would wonder what he had done.

He thought about Janice. She was always concerned about what other people thought about them. She was worried anything they did that wasn't the right thing would jeopardize her business. She was especially concerned about what the people in the neighborhood thought. She had hosted several dinner parties and barbeques to make sure they knew them, liked them and most of all, they knew about her business. It was one of her ways to promote her flower shop. If the police came to the house it could hurt everything she had worked for.

His mind continued to race. He thought, *I can put the money in a suitcase and take it to the police station. I can tell them what happened. I have no record. They would believe me. But maybe they would interrogate me. I would have to drive the car to the station. Maybe someone is watching. They would follow me. Maybe kill me for the money.*

Something came to him. He began to figure it out. The money was delivered to the wrong address. For sure the Mexican dropped off the money and thought he was someone else. *But why me*, he thought.

The man didn't demand anything. If he came here with that kind of money, you'd think he would be picking up drugs. It had to be. There had been so many reports of drugs coming from Mexico, Fred figured that's what it had to be. His mind was racing. His head began to hurt.

His thoughts continued to fill his head. So, if he didn't ask for something in return, it either had to be debt for work done or someone was coming to pick it up. They had used his house as a safe house. But why his house? Again, his thoughts turned to the fact the Mexican had delivered the money to the wrong place. Someone was coming to pick it up. He had to have a plan. He had to come up with something.

Fred grabbed an old suitcase and stuffed the money inside. He figured what to do with it. When he bought the house from a divorcee, he was told there was a hole inside the garage behind two large metal storage cabinets. He learned that was where the husband had stored his collection of porno movies and books, one of the reasons for the divorce.

He had seen the storage hole one time before. He was surprised to see so many CDs and magazines had been left behind. He didn't throw them away. To kill time the past few weeks, Fred had watched several of the movies.

He dragged the case to the garage, pulled back the cabinet and stuffed the case inside the opening. It just fit. He closed the cabinet and walked back into his office. He would sit and wait for whoever was coming to pick up the money. But then he figured nobody would be coming. The money was either delivered to the wrong address or the right address at the wrong street. His mind became active again. It was time to call Janice. It was time to get out. Two million ideas ran though his mind. Where? He wasn't sure. But it didn't take long for a place to appear: the South of France. He picked up the phone. Then put it down. He decided it was best not to call her. He showered, dressed, packed a suitcase and would wait for her to come home. He would then surprise her with a trip.

Another thought raced through his mind. 'If the Mexican dropped off the money to the wrong house, then the person who was going to pick it up would go to the right house which would be the wrong house. That would give him time. Time for what? He wasn't sure.

Truth was, Fred's mind was scrambled. He didn't know what to do. A thought came to him. He would take the money, stuff it in a sports bag, drive to the flower shop, pick up Janice and drive to the airport. He shook his head and laughed to himself. She couldn't just pick up and go. She would need to come back to the house and pack. And maybe the Mexican would figure out he delivered the money to the wrong house and there could be people waiting for him. He couldn't let Janice get involved in what happened. He had to wait until she got home and get her to agree to take off on a trip.

Fred peeked out the front window. The street looked empty. There wasn't one car parked on the street. Even the driveways were empty. He knew that's the way it was every day. He decided to open the door. He stopped. *They could be watching for me.* He dropped his head down. He told himself to take it easy. He had to relax and come up with a plan. He threw his hands up in the air. He almost called out. He didn't have a clue what to do.

Thirty-two

Sue was on her way to the house. She repeated the address in her mind; 11646 El Camino Real. Again and again.

She kept reaching inside her purse and running her fingers over the .38 pistol. She had fallen in love with it after Mat had taken her to a firing range. She loved the feel of the gun in her hand. She loved the sound it made and the little jolt when she pulled the trigger. She loved the smell of the fire and smoke.

She found the street. She saw the house. "Very nice...wow."

Sue sat in the car for a few minutes and looked up and down the street. She couldn't remember ever being in a neighborhood like this. She never had been.

She was mesmerized by the rows of beautiful homes and the well-kept gardens and yards. She twisted her head in all directions and smiled to herself. She stared at the different designs. The large two-story houses caught her eye. The tan color and the red roofs seem to shine in the early morning sun. She thought how quiet it was.

She thought about where she had lived growing up. She had spent the most of her life in an apartment in a small town. She lived with her mom and dad. Her mother was seldom home, and Sue learned early on to make it on her own. She had told Mat her story but left out several details. She never told him she left home when she was sixteen, went to Myrtle Beach and hustled men for a place to eat, sleep and clean up. She never took money. They had to settle for a blow job or nothing. She never considered herself a whore. When she was eighteen, she found her way to Atlanta. She had been an exotic dancer ever since.

Sue emerged from the car, grabbed her purse and walked toward the large house. She had dressed in a very short and tight pair of jean shorts and a white halter top. She had left her bra at home. She wore spiked heels.

She rang the doorbell. Within a few seconds a man opened the door. He looked at her and said, "You can't be the fucking delivery boy. That's for sure."

Sue studied him for a minute. He was tall, over six feet, with short blond hair and a round stomach. She said, "Delivery? No. Pickup."

The man's head moved up and down, taking in the full view. He gave her a wicked smile. He remembered Fat Baby told him a lady was going to make the pickup. He wanted to make sure this was the right one. He said, "You're telling me you came here for a pickup. Pick up what? Garbage?"

"You going to let me in or not? It's kind of hot, you know."

"Sure. Sure. Come on in."

Charlie glanced down at Sue's ass as she strutted into the house. She looked around. "Nice house from the outside. But inside. Not too cool."

"I live alone. I don't need a bunch of shit. A lounger, TV and booze. What the fuck else do I need? Huh?"

Sue stood in the middle of the living room. She turned around. "Let's do this quickly and get it over with. Where's the package?"

"Wait. Just wait. You're telling me you're here for the pickup. Get out."

"Don't fuck with me. I don't think Fat Baby would be very happy with you talking to me like that."

"He sent you, huh? He sent a hot chick to pick up the money. He said he was sending a woman, but...wow. He's the man. For a second

I thought you were from an escort service going door to door selling your—"

She cut him off. "Did you say money?"

"Yeah...money. Lots of it. What? You're the pickup and you don't know what you're supposed to pick up."

"I know now. How much?"

Charlie laughed. "Jesus, what kind of deal is this? I'm supposed to hand over two million large to you and you don't—"

Sue shouted, "Two million dollars! Are you shitting me?"

Charlie walked over and plopped down on the lounger. He pulled on the handle and the chair flipped up. "Well, now you know. You might as well sit and relax. It ain't here."

"It was supposed to be here at eight. I was to be here at nine. It's six after nine. Get the money and I'm out of here."

"I said it hasn't come."

Sue walked over to the chair and leaned over, making sure he would get a good look at her soft breasts. "I'm getting a message here. You figure...what the hell is this? I give this little girl a line of bullshit. She leaves and I'm on my way with two mil."

Charlie gave her breasts a long look. He leaned back and said, "I'm going to say it again. It has not arrived. So, if you want to wait, sit and relax. Or maybe you'd like to mess around some. I got some meth, baby. We could get—"

Sue leaned closer and placed her fingers on his lips. "Get the fucking money. 'Cause if you don't, I make a call and you'll be dead before I hang up."

Charlie shook his head and laughed. "Tough girl, huh? Get out of my face."

Sue reached in her purse, rolled her fingers around the trigger, yanked the gun out and placed it to the side of Charlie's head. She said softly, "Now, asshole, stand up slowly. Come on...get up."

His head snapped back. It was the first time in his life someone had pointed a gun at him. He mumbled, "Take it easy. I..."

Sue was enjoying the action. She snapped, "I said. Get up. Slowly. And don't try to be a hero. I want you to know I shot my stepfather three times when he tried to rape me. I kind of liked it."

Charlie stood. His whole body shook. She said, "Take off your belt." She watched as he did. "Now, let's walk over to that kitchen chair. You sit and put your hands behind the chair. And don't move. Bang!" she shouted.

He let out a small squeal, jumped two feet and then stumbled toward the chair. He sat and put his hands. Sue remembered a little thing Mat had showed her. She wrapped the belt around the back of the chair and around his hands. She pulled tight, twisted it around and tied it tight.

"Tell me where you have some heavy-duty tape. And don't bullshit me. All men have that kind of shit."

"Top drawer. Over there." He nodded toward a row of drawers.

Sue walked over keeping the gun pointed at him. She opened a drawer and found a large roll of gray tape. She walked back and wrapped the tape around his hands and belt. She then tied one leg at a time to the chair.

She stood back. "Now. Where is the fucking money?"

"Come on," Charlie shouted, "It's not here. Whoever was to make the drop must be late."

"I'm pissed." She grabbed the tape and began wrapping it around his chest and the chair. She moved around the table and sat in one of the other chairs.

They sat in silence. She kept looking at her watch. She should be on her way back to her place. They had timed the trip. She was already running late. She had to do something.

"Think about it. You think I would fuck over Fat Baby? He'd find me and kill me before I could spend a penny. He set this whole thing up. The money was coming from Mexico delivered to me by one of his delivery boys. A cat named Hector—"

Sue smirked. "Wait? A cat? Did you say a cat?"

"I dunno know. Jesus, you put a gun to my head, tied me up and... okay some Mexican dude. What I am trying to say is he never showed."

"Did you call Fat Baby and tell him? It's been an hour."

"He told me not to call him. You got to know this guy. He's hung up on trust and keeping anonymous. He put this whole plan together to make sure other people handle the money until he's sure it's safe and then he'll have you...or whomever you're working for, deliver the money. He doesn't want to hear from anyone until then."

Suddenly something came to her. She stood and laughed out loud. "What the hell am I thinking? Two million big ones are making my mind get all fucked up. Am I asleep or what?"

"Now what" Charlie asked.

She moved around in front of him. She stood there for a second and then ripped her blouse off over her head. She slid down on his lap. She shoved her breasts into his face. "Let's work this out. I'm not greedy. I'll take five hundred thousand. You take the rest."

Charlie was caught off guard. Her breasts pounded his face and he could feel her legs rubbing up against him. She began to twist and grind her body over his. "Come on, man. Get it. And I'll give you an extra surprise and we're out of here."

"Oh, man. You're fucking me up. You got to believe me. It never came. Somebody ran off with it. Hell, if I had it I would gladly give you some...and for a chance to fuck you. Hell, I might give you all if it."

Sue continued to grind on his lap. She had to make sure. She hadn't met too many men who wouldn't jump at the chance to have sex with her. She pressed her lips to his ear. "Listen, I'm not an idiot. I know how much two mil is, but you can have it. Just throw me a bone and..." she laughed, "I mean five hundred large and then you can throw me a large bone of your own. I decided it was time for me to make it on my own. Don't be a jerk."

"You're not getting this. If I were going to take the fucking money, do you think I would have waited for someone to come and pick it up? I would have left ten seconds after the money was dropped off. Jesus, use your head."

Sue jumped up and put on her top. She believed him. She grabbed her cell. She called Mat. "You got to get over here. This asshole is telling me the money never came. He's tied up. I held the gun to his head and rolled my tits in his face and promised him a good fuck. He turned it down...he ain't lying."

Thirty-three

The two men drove slowly down El Camino Real. One was an American and the other a Mexican. They spotted the address clearly marked on the mailbox post. All the houses had the same boxes with the addresses on the posts. The American was driving. He looked over to his partner and said, "There's the house. I don't feel comfortable parking on this street. Look as these houses. Nicely built but in a way ticky-tacky. And not one fucking car on the street. Everybody must have left for work or everybody parks their cars in their garages."

"Maybe there is some kind of ordinance that they can't park on the street...like at night or something."

"Could be." The American continued to drive down the street. His head was moving from side to side looking for somewhere to park. He pointed, "Look. There's a little park over there. There are a few parking spaces. We'll be able to see the house from there."

"Just as long as some mothers don't bring their kids to the park. It would not be cool for us."

"We'll see." He backed in to one of the spaces and turned off the engine. "Now we wait."

"What's the drill?" the Mexican asked.

"We are just to observe and follow...and we can't be recognized. When the pickup is made, The Captain will tell us what to do."

It didn't take long for a car to pull up in front of the house and stop. They watched as Sue got out of the car and walked toward the door. The Mexican said, "There. Look. Oh, man, look at that outfit. Look at that ass. Nice long legs, too."

"She must be the pickup."

"I'd like to pick her up."

They watched as the door opened and she went inside. The Mexican said, "I think maybe we make a move. Get the money and give the lady a good fucking and head to the airport. We can be in Mexico before anybody knows."

The American laughed. "Yeah. And dead before we could spend a dollar. Every drug dealer in Mexico would be notified and coming after us. They wouldn't hesitate to cut off our balls and stuff them down our throat."

~ * ~

It wasn't too long before another car pulled up and parked behind Sue's car. They watched as a man got out of the car and trotted toward the door. The American turned toward the Mexican. "Something's not right. I don't like this."

"You think something went wrong with the pickup?"

"First the lady goes in and, well, she's been in there too long. Now this dude shows up."

"Think maybe they killed the man inside and are taking the money?"

"I don't know."

"Should be call The Captain?"

"Let's wait a few minutes and see what goes down. Maybe she called for backup. Hell, I don't have clue."

~ * ~

Mat walked into the kitchen. He looked at the man taped to the chair. "What the hell?"

Sue smiled and said, "You taught me this. Cool, huh?"

Mat walked over and ripped the tape from the man's mouth. He yelled out. Mat said, "So, either you haven't received the money, or you have a death wish."

"Why doesn't anyone want to believe me?" he replied. He stopped for a second then shouted, "The fucking money never came. Get it?"

Mat crossed his arms. "Okay, relax. Take it easy."

"Your lady friend is a little nuts, you know. Waving that gun in my face and all."

"Listen, she came here to pick up the money. You're supposed to have it. What did you expect her to do? Say, okay I believe you. Bye."

"I just didn't expect this. That's all I'm saying. And then your lady friend here rubs her tits in my face and offers me a good fuck if I give her five hundred grand."

Mat turned and looked at Sue. "You did that? You were going take off?"

Sue didn't hesitate. "Jesus, Mat. It was just a plan to get the bastard to give me the money. You know I would have called you, grabbed it and headed home. I thought maybe I should put what God gave me to good use."

Charlie yelled, "She's so full of shit. She was all over me and..."

Mat sat down across from him. "Just shut up, okay. Let's go over this. First, who are you and why did Fat Baby choose you for the delivery?"

"I'm Charlie. I am a tax accountant. I do the books and taxes for him. He trusts me. He knows I wouldn't take the money. He's paying me enough."

"Yeah, his favorite word. Trust. So, how much is he paying you for this trust?"

"Fifty large."

"And you wouldn't be tempted to take the entire two mil?"

"I'd be dead before I spend it. Fat Baby's got people everywhere. I'm happy with the fifty big ones. I have a ticket to Vegas. I was supposed to be on my way to the airport. I was hoping to have a wild time in Vegas with my cash. You know, what happens in Vegas..."

"I know. I know. Here's the deal. We're going to rip this place apart. And...do you have the fifty grand?"

"What? No. I was to take it out of the two mil."

Mat sighed and rubbed his hands through his hair. He took a swing at Charlie and drove his fist into the side of his face. Charlie's head snapped back. He screamed in pain. Mat took a step back and drove his foot into Charlie's ribs. Again, he screamed.

Charlie rolled his head around trying to catch his breath. "What the hell is that for?"

"Insurance. Just making sure you know we mean business."

"You got to believe me."

"Maybe I do. Maybe I don't. This whole trust thing with Fat Baby. He's big on it. He wouldn't have chosen you if he thought for a second you would take it and run."

"Like he chose you...and who are you?"

"Not important. What is important is...who has the fucking money?"

Mat looked deep into Charlie's eyes. He believed him. "We can all sit around and wait. But if you're telling the truth, and I think you are, you would have been long gone before we came."

"Thank you. Now—"

Mat cut him off. "Here's the deal. We're leaving. I'm not going to take the time right now to trash this place. I need to do some work and find out what happened to the person who was to deliver the money. If we find him, maybe we can figure this out. We're keeping you like this. And—"

Charlie shouted, "Ah, come on. Take this fucking tape off me."

"Can't do. But we won't tape your mouth. You won't scream 'cause you wouldn't want the neighbors to see you like this. Plus, you need to stay here until we figure this out."

"Shit."

"Let me say this, Charlie my boy, if you're lying you won't have to worry about Fat Baby. A guy showed me something once. He said there's a part of the brain you can fire a bullet into. And it won't kill the person. It will make the person a vegetable for the rest of his life.

You want to be that person, Charlie? You want to be a vegetable, huh, do you, Charlie?"

Charlie could hardly catch his breath. He tried to speak. He mumbled. "Oh, shit. You got to believe me."

"We'll see, pal. Now, where's your cell phone?"

"On my desk in my office."

"Sue, go get it."

Sue left and came back in a few minutes. "I took his laptop, too. And this thing here...his hand held...something."

"Okay, Charlie, hang tight. We'll be back when we figure this out."

"At least let me have drink of water. There's a bottle in the fridge."

Sue opened the door and took out a bottle of water. She turned the cap and walked over to Charlie. He opened his mouth and she squirted the water deep into his mouth.

"Thanks...and by the way, nice tits. They seemed real. Are they?"

Mat closed his eyes and shook his head. Sue laughed, "Stop by The Pink Lady and I'll give you a special show. And, yes, they are real."

Mat and Sue walked to the door. Mat said, "Would you have fucked him?"

"For two mil, I'd fuck the Pope."

"Would you have taken the money and run?"

"Trust...remember?"

Mat shook his head again and headed toward the car.

Thirty-four

"I have to call Fat Baby." Mat fumbled for his phone.

"So, Charlie was right."

"Not important."

"Fat Baby is a drug dealer. Everybody knows who his is. What's going on, Mat? That's bad shit. You're a cop. Wait...wait...it's a sting. Oh God, how cool. I'm part of a sting. You deliver the money to the fat man and bam, the SWAT team moves in."

Mat looked over at Sue and smiled. He would let her believe her story.

Mat punched in Fat Baby's number. He answered on the first ring. "Talk to me, Mat. Better be important. I asked you not to call unless—"

"We just left the pickup house. The money never arrived."

There was dead silence. Mat continued, "Before you go ballistic. I believe your man. The money wasn't there."

"Mat, don't be doing this. I have to believe my man dropped off the money."

"Fat Baby...trust, remember? I know what you're thinking already. But don't. I would gain nothing by taking the money. It would only cause me to be dead. And I have fifty good reasons to play it straight. I wouldn't be calling you if I had the money. I would be long gone by now."

"Okay...trust. I trust you and you believe the man and the money never got to him."

"I do. If he took it, he's would have been gone long before we got there. And holding a gun to someone's head usually works. Plus, he's a little tied up now. If he's that good of a liar and the money is there, then he won't be going anywhere. And if we find out the money, if fact, was delivered, I'll come back and deal with him."

"I believe the money never came. He can be trusted as I trust you. I hope my trusting isn't going to cost me two million. You know it's not about the money. It's about this whole thing with my new partners and, of course, trust. Do you have any ideas?"

"I am on way to the place where Hector works."

"Just can't believe he would take a chance on keeping the money."

"He is Mexican. And who knows how deep he can hide out in the desert? You know, lay low for a while."

"Yeah, but he also knows I would do whatever it took or how long it took to cut off his nuts."

"I'll find him and get back to you."

Sue looked over at Mat. "You and Fat Baby; best buddies. You got him believing you're going to hand over the money. He'll be in for some surprise."

"We got to find it first."

"I got a feeling you're not going to rest until you find it, all right. And I'm going to be right by your side."

"I think it's best I take you back to your place, but you know, it would take some time to do that and we don't have much."

"I'm in. Get it?"

"We'll see. It could be dangerous. I might not have a choice. I can't risk a civilian in this type of operation."

She reached in her purse, pulled out her weapon and shouted, "Bang. Bang."

~ * ~

"I guess we need to follow them," the Mexican said.

"For sure. Nothing seems to be going according to plan. They should have walked out with a large case full of money."

The car slowly drove out of the parking space and into the flow of traffic. The American said, "I'm going to call The Captain."

"He doesn't like to be called."

"I know. But we got to know what to do."

"I would suggest we keep up the observation like we've been told. No use causing a problem before we know if there is one."

~ * ~

Fat Baby called Bones. "Get a partner and go over to the address we talked about. There's a guy there tied up. He says our delivery boy never showed up. Make sure he's telling the truth. And remember, trust."

Thirty-five

Mat drove to West End Nursery and Landscaping. He pulled up and said, "I'm going inside. Wait here."

"No way. I said I'm in."

Mat scratched his head. "Come on. Jesus."

They walked into the office. A man was standing behind a long high counter studying a stack of papers. He looked up. "Hey. Can I help you?"

"Looking for Hector Morales."

"Never heard of him."

"Right. He works here."

"Who's looking for him?"

Mat snapped, "A friend."

"He doesn't have any friends."

"Who are you?" Mat snapped.

"Who the hell are you?" the man snapped back.

"You know, I wanted to make this easy. Just tell me where he's working today, and I'll be on my way."

"We don't give out information about our employees to strangers."

"I like that. But, in this case you'll have to make an exception. Name's Mat..."

"Wait. I know who you are. I just needed a few minutes to remember. You're a cop. You busted in here a few years ago, thinking you were going to make a big-time arrest. And you couldn't find one illegal Mexican."

"Good for you. Now, where's Hector?"

"He's legal. Good-bye."

"Okay, here's the deal. This is official police business. Don't be playing games with me. Legal or illegal, I'll make your life miserable."

The man didn't respond. Mat snapped, "You know, I'm running out of time. Where is he working?"

The man turned and looked at Sue. "You can't be a cop. You must be a friend of Hector's, too?"

"I can't be. You said he didn't have any."

"Funny. Real funny."

"Come on, man. Just give me the information," Mat said.

"He's in trouble, I know. What'd he do?"

Mat closed his eyes and shook his head. "Tell me, what's your name and what is your job here?"

"Andy. I manage the company."

"Good. Now Andy, where is the owner?"

"We are owned by a large company out of Houston. Be honest, I don't even know the executives. I just get a paycheck like everyone else."

"Okay, Andy, we're getting somewhere." Mat leaned over the counter and raised his voice, "Where the fuck is he?"

"He called in sick. He hasn't missed a day in years and today he called in sick."

Mat turned toward Sue. He gave her a funny look. He turned back to Andy. "Give me his address in Juarez."

Mat grabbed the slip of paper from Andy and they left and drove hard toward the border. "It doesn't look good for Hector."

"You're thinking he never showed up and took the money and ran."

"I just can't believe he would do that. But, shit, it looks that way."

"Maybe he was followed, and someone took the money. Maybe he's already dead."

"Too many maybes. Let's hope we find him...alive."

Mat stopped at the border and talked to one of the guards he knew. He was told Hector had passed through early that morning as usual. He thanked the officer and got directions to Hector's house. He got back into the car. He looked over at Sue. "We're being tagged. I'm going to stop at the little store over there. I want you to come inside with me."

"What are you going to do?"

"Just do it."

They walked into the store. Mat found the back door and worked his way to the back of the car. He approached the driver side and tapped on the window. The man inside jerked his head back. Mat motioned for him to put his window down. The window came down. Mat said, "Hi there. Seems like you're following me. And you know what, I don't like that."

"And what the fuck would make you think we're following you?"

"Because I'm not stupid. You are. Now, here's the deal. I don't care why. Really, I don't." Mat pulled his sport coat back revealing his weapon hanging from its holster. He continued, "But, when I drive out of here and you follow me, I am going to pull next to you and empty my magazine in your fucking heads. And you know what, when the Mexican police come, they'll say it was just another drug gang war. And you'll be dead, and they won't give a shit. Now, have a nice day...and go home...alive."

Mat walked back to his car, opened the door and got in. Sue had found her way back to the car. "I don't think they work for Fat Baby. I think the Mexicans are planning something. Like getting their money back and screwing him. You know what, that's not my concern. We need to find Hector."

"Are they going to follow us anymore?"

"I think I shook them up a little. They'll be heading back across the border."

~ * ~

The American turned to his partner. "Make the call. We need to know what to do. Jesus, who is that dude?"

"I can't get a signal. Try your cell."

"I don't have it with me. I left it on the kitchen table. Keep trying."

"It's no use. Turn around and drive back into El Paso. We can call from there."

They drove through the border. The Mexican said, "You really left your cell at home? I sleep with this thing. Jesus, you left it at home. That's funny. You know how much we rely on these things."

"Just drop it, okay. Make the call."

"Sir, this is Raul. We were spotted by the pickup man. He said if we continue to follow him, he would blow us away. He had a Glock hanging from a shoulder holster."

"Where are you?"

In El Paso. Just inside the border. We couldn't get a signal down there."

The man thought for a minute. He said, "What kind of car does he drive?"

"A red Mustang convertible with a black top. An older model. It has a dent in the driver's side. In the back."

"Come on in. I'll take it from here."

The man made a call, instructed two very good Mexicans in Juarez and gave them a description of the car. He told them to locate the car and continue to observe but not to be noticed.

Thirty-six

Sue sat quietly, running different ideas through her head as Mat drove to Hector's house. Something seemed out of sorts. She looked over at Mat and said, "This is getting very exciting. I think I'm getting turned on. What kind of deal did you make with Fat Baby?"

Mat continued the charade. "I worked my way into his operation through Jamar. He liked the fact I was a cop. To him, a bad cop. He offered me fifty thou to do this."

"So, Fat Baby's giving you fifty grand for this. In my mind that's way, way too much money just for picking it up. And if you do this and he gets arrested, he could come after you, you know."

"That's the life of a cop. What can I say? If I worried about all the people I've arrested coming after me, I'd be bald by now."

Sue smiled, "You know I did notice a few thin spots."

Mat looked over at her. He thought for a second. What she didn't know was Baby was paying him for more than just picking up the money. He wanted to own him. He knew then he was in too deep. It was time to get out. Get out with two million.

Mat decided it was time to tell her what was going to happen. "What would you think about coming with me to a little town in Mexico right on the Gulf? A place called LaPaz?"

"Not quite sure what you mean. After this is over, we go for a vacation in...where? Las..."

"LaPaz. But not a vacation. How about maybe a lifetime?"

"You mean...holy shit...take the money and run. You got to be crazy. Fat Baby will find us, and we won't have a second to spend a dime."

"I'm willing to take that chance."

Sue looked over at Mat. "You're serious. You really believe you can hide from him."

"I know this place. It's a villa right on the beach. I've been there. It will be hard for anyone to find us. Plus, we can stay there for a while and then maybe go somewhere else."

Sue jumped up and down in her seat. She yelled, "Two million? Well, screw it. I'm in."

~ * ~

Hector approached the border station. He slowed down and drove into the lane he always took. It was early. He wondered if the border guard would be curious. He would be surprised to see him so early in the morning.

He pulled up to the gate. The guard looked into the car. "Hector. You are early. Hey, you didn't get fired, did you?"

Hector faked a small smile. "Na. I bent down and I get light headed and go down for the count."

"It was the bear, man. The bear can get you some time."

Hector nodded and waved as the guard opened the gate. For the first time all day he felt relaxed. He never had been so nervous. Now all he wanted to do was collect the money they had promised him for making the delivery and go home. He was told that delivery would be his last.

As he drove to the house, he had visited earlier that morning he couldn't help thinking about the look on the man's face when he popped open his shirt and dropped his pants. It was almost like he didn't know he was coming. The more Hector thought about it, the more he had the feeling something wasn't right. He had expected the man to be all over him and anxious to be getting the money. But then he thought the man was as nervous as he was and just wanted to get it over with.

He drove up to the front of the house, parked and walked up to the front door. He looked around at the street. The street was empty. He knocked. Nobody answered. He knocked harder. He called out. There was no response. He tried looking into the windows, but they were blacked out.

Hector walked back to his car. He kept looking back over his shoulder to see if anybody had come to the door. He thought he remembered he was supposed to come back to the house after the drop-off and show them the piece of paper with the man's signature on it. Or maybe he was supposed to take the money out of one of the pockets. For a minute, he became confused. He started to walk back to the house. He wanted to find out if what he remembered was true. Everything had happened so fast and he was so confused and anxious in the morning, maybe he hadn't heard what he was to do to get his money.

He started up the small set of stairs when a Juarez police car pulled up behind his. The officer got out and called out. "Hey. Hey there. Where are you going?"

Hector was caught off guard. He could feel a hot bolt of heat flash throughout his body. He turned. "Me?"

"Yes. You. What are you doing here?"

Hector thought quickly. "I came to visit a friend."

The police officer moved toward him. Hector had no idea what to expect. The police officer called out, "What is your name?"

"Hector. Hector Morales."

"Hector. This house has been abandoned for months. Nobody lives here. You have an ID on you?"

Hector could hardly speak. He couldn't believe what the man had said. He had been there a few hours earlier. He stammered, "Yes." He reached in his back pocket and pulled out his wallet. He handed it to the officer and said, "I...I...came to visit...Jose. An old friend."

The officer studied his driver's license. He handed the wallet back to Hector. "Several months ago, there was a call that someone had heard what they thought was the sound of gun fire. When we got here a man was found shot to death. I don't think his name was Jose."

"I...I...don't know anything about that. It's been awhile since I was here."

The officer studied Hector for a few minutes. He asked, "You work here in Juarez?"

"No, sir. I work in El Paso at a landscaping company. I have my green card and—"

"Okay," the officer said and began to walk back to his car. "Maybe you should try to find your friend. I hope it wasn't the man who was killed."

Hector waved and scampered back to his car. He got inside and took a second to collect himself. His hands were shaking, and his head was pounding. The only thing he could think about was how he was going to get his money. His other thought was next Tuesday the money would be in his truck like always. But that was never mentioned. As he started the car, he thought to himself, *they have my cell phone. I can't even call anybody.* Then he laughed out loud and said, "I wouldn't have anybody to call anyways."

~ * ~

Mat found a dirt road with several small houses on it. He spotted Hector in the front of his house washing his truck. He pulled up next to the truck and got out of the car. Sue followed.

Hector looked surprised and confused as Mat walked toward him. Mat called out, "Hey, Hector, what's up?"

"Not much. Just giving the ol' truck a good cleaning."

"Heard you called in sick. You all right?"

Hector felt another jolt of heat pass through his body. He stammered, "You...you talked to my boss...why?"

"Oh, I just wanted to talk to you for a few minutes, so we dropped by the nursery."

"What about?"

"By the way, this is Sue."

Hector nodded. Mat continued, "Think we could find a quiet place to maybe have a drink and lunch. You know...an outside café?"

Again, Hector wasn't sure what was going on and he stuttered, "I...I guess. Let me change and—"

"You're fine. Come on."

Mat waited for Hector to take a few steps toward the car and Mat slipped in behind him. Sue followed.

Hector turned his head around. "Anything wrong?"

"We'll talk when we get there." Mat handed Hector the keys. "You drive."

Ten minutes later they were sitting at a table at the end of the café. The place was almost empty. Mat ordered two margaritas and a double shot of tequila for himself. Hector was quiet and nervous. He never knew what to expect from Mat.

Their drinks arrived and all of them took long swigs. Mat drained his shot and slammed the glass on the table. He said, "Whoa. Good stuff."

Hector said, "So, why the visit?"

"Hector, let me say you always delivered for me. You always had my money ready for me. And I value that in you. Everything I've heard about you has been good stuff. Words like trusting and loyal and...well, you know."

"I have always been. You know that."

Mat leaned over and whispered, "Then why in the fuck didn't you deliver the money this morning?"

Hector's head snapped back. It was the last thing he expected to hear. His eyes opened wide and said, "I...and how...what's going on, wait...how would you...no wait, I made the drop off. I was there at eight a.m. sharp. Mat, I'm confused with all this. Talk to me."

"First, let me say, me and Sue went to the house to pick up the money and deliver it to Fat Baby."

"You? Man, oh man. You work for him? Wait...I see it. You contacted him after you made a deal with me."

"Not important. What is important is you're fucking with the wrong people. We went to the house. The man did not have the money."

"Mat, he had to. I gave it to him...look." Hector reached in his back pocket and pulled out a piece of paper. "He signed this." He handed it to Mat.

Mat looked at it. "This is nothing but chicken scratching. It's unreadable."

"I didn't look at it. All I did was ask him to sign where it said accepted."

Sue leaned forward and said, "Hector I was there at nine. I went there first. I held a gun to the man's head. I even offered him...never mind. Let's just say he was scared shitless. If he had the money, he sure played it cool. Mat came later, and we worked him over pretty well. I have to believe he ain't got the money."

"But I was there."

"Tell me everything. Every detail."

"Let me see. I went to a house in town early this morning. Under my clothes a man taped on this white silk like suit with little pockets filled with money. They gave me a GPS. I typed in the address in my cell and drove to El Paso. I was scared, man. I was hurtin'. But I made it. Got to the house, walked in, stripped off my shirt, dropped my pants to my knees and ripped off the suit. The man signed this paper and I left. It took me less than ten minutes... maybe less. I called in sick, drove back here and I've been waiting for my money."

Mat waved his hand in the air and called out for another round. He sat there silently waiting for the drinks. After they arrived, he yanked the glass to his mouth and drained the liquor. He looked over at Sue. "Not drinking?"

"You know, I believe this guy," she said.

"I don't know who to believe. But I do know someone is lying big time." He tapped his fingers on the table. "Let me think...let me...the GPS must still be on your phone. You have it?"

"Sure. In my truck."

"I suggest we get the GPS, get in the car and follow the directions. Let's see where it took you."

~ * ~

The two Mexicans spotted the red Mustang with the black top and dent as it sped toward the border station. The driver positioned the car in the lane next to the Mustang. They both were cleared through customs about the same time. The Mexican pushed the car in front of the Mustang. They were on their way.

Thirty-seven

Bones and his partner, Lamar, walked into the house. He shouted, "Anybody home?"

Charlie called out, "Here. In the kitchen."

They walked into the kitchen. Bones burst out laughing. "My, my, look at this. The man is all taped up. You look like a mummy."

"Not so funny. And who are you?"

"Doesn't matter."

"You going to get me out of this shit?"

"Not yet. Tell us where the money is, and I'll think about it."

"Ah, Jesus. Here we go again. Like I told the last dude and his hotter than hot lady, the money never made it here."

"You're saying someone came to pick up the money?"

"I just said that."

"And it was a lady and some dude?"

"What is this? Twenty questions?"

"Just answer me."

"Some hot babe came here at nine. She wouldn't believe me. Nobody believes me. She put me in this strait jacket, held a gun to my head and offered me...never mind. I told her I never got the money.

Then she called some dude. He came. Smashed my face a few times. Kicked me in the fucking ribs. They looked around and left me like this." He cleared his throat and yelled, "I never got the money. Some Mexican is running around with two mil and people are beating me up."

"Cool. Mind if we look around?"

"Listen. I just want this to end. I may not be a genius, but I wouldn't fuck with Fat Baby. Look, I got a ticket to Vegas. But because of all this shit I missed my flight. He was paying me fifty grand. Why for the life of me would I want to take his money?"

Bones laughed out loud. "I could think of two million reasons. See, that kind of money makes people do strange things."

Charlie lowered his head and shook it from side to side. "I'm hungry. I want to get up, get some food and forget this ever happened. Just take this tape off me."

Bones turned toward Lamar. "Let's look around."

Bones grabbed a large kitchen knife and walked into the living room. He started the search by tearing up the sofa. He and his partner tossed, ripped and turned the living room upside down, then proceeded to the man's office. They turned the entire room upside down and found nothing. They found the bedroom. They did the same to the bedroom. They sifted through the closet, tossing clothes everywhere. They emptied every drawer and ripped the bed apart. Again, they found nothing. They tore the rest of the house apart.

Bones pulled open the air conditioner vent and reached inside. He walked back into the living room and found one packed suitcase. He opened it and tore through the clothes. He found nothing. The two men stood in the middle of the mess. "Let's go to the garage," Bones said.

They walked back into the kitchen and toward the garage door. "Look. Keys are hanging here. I'll check the car."

Ten minutes later they returned to the kitchen. Bones called out, "Pal, if the money's here, it sure is hidden good."

Charlie cried out, "The delivery man never came. Will somebody believe me and cut me loose?"

"Charlie, my man, whoever did this had a reason. And I'm sure they'll be back. But since I like you, and if we solve this and you're clean, I'll come back and cut you loose, and take you to dinner."

"I'm guessing you work for Fat Baby. So, do me a favor and call him and tell him I never got the money and get me out of this shit."

"Have a great day, pal." Bones and his partner left the house.

Thirty-eight

Mat and Sue waited while Hector went into his house. His mind was racing. He walked over to the other side of his car and made a call. A man answered. "Eugene. It's Mat. Listen. I need a new convertible. Red. Got one?"

"Hey, Mat. You're finally going to get rid of that relic."

"Yeah. How much for a new one?"

"I got one on the lot. Thirty-five grand. I'll give you a grand—"

"Never mind. I'm going to have a lady friend of mind come over this afternoon. She'll have the cash. Have the paperwork ready. She's in and out in record time. Keep my car. Title's in the glove compartment. It's yours. Do what you want with it. And there's five grand in it for you in an envelope. Can you do it?"

"Consider it done."

"Make sure the title is in her name and that's it."

He walked back and stood next to Sue. "Here's the deal. I know this guy at El Paso Ford. His name is Eugene. He used to be a cop. Now he sells cars. He's going to have a new red Mustang convertible ready. When we get the money, we'll drive to your place. You take the car and drive to the dealership. He'll know what to do. The car will be waiting."

"Cool."

Hector closed the door and jogged toward the car. They got in and were on their way.

Mat pushed the old Mustang hard on Interstate 10. He listened to the voice on the GPS. Sue sat next to him and Hector sat in the back seat. From time to time Sue would hold up her pistol and point it at him. Hector kept telling her he didn't like guns and to put it away.

Matt followed the directions specifically. Within the hour, they were turning onto El Camino Real. Mat slowed as he approached the house, he had left a few hours earlier. The voice on the GPS said, "You're approaching your destination." Mat slowed down. He pulled up in front of the house. The voice said, "Proceed for one thousand feet to your destination."

Mat looked at the screen. The address read 11664 El Camino Real. It didn't take long for him to figure it out. He yelled out, "Holy shit, Hector, you flip-flopped the last two numbers and went to the wrong house. Goddamn, you should have dropped off the money at one-one-six-four-six. You punched in one-one-four-six-four. The house you went to is a few houses down the street."

Mat grabbed the GPS and threw it in the back seat, barely missing Hector. He said, "Let me think for a minute."

Sue couldn't stop laughing. "Oh, God. This is a riot. We went to the right house which in this case is the wrong house, and the guy in there is taped to a chair. Mat, I need to go in there and cut him loose."

"Let's make sure first. We need to go to the house down the street and I'm going to knock on the door. When the man answers, Hector you sit in the car, stay low get a good look and give me a sign that it's the right guy. Make sure he doesn't see you. Sue, you take off and walk back and take care of...of...Charlie. Here, give him a couple hundred and apologize. But nothing more. I think you like this guy...maybe too much."

Sue gave him a funny look and said sarcastically, "Ha. Ha."

Thirty-nine

Bones made the call. Fat Baby answered. "What is going on, Bones?"

"I'm not sure. Who did you send to pick up the money?"

"Not important. What is important is what did you find out?"

"Your boy was tied to a chair. He was knocked around a bit. He said a woman came in and then a man came, after he told her he never got the money."

"You believe him?"

"We kind of tore the house apart. We even looked in his car and in the garage. If he's lying and the money's in that house, well…"

"I have to make a few calls and find out where the Mexican who was supposed to deliver the money lives. Hang loose. 'Cause when I find out, I want you to get down to Juarez and find the bastard. And if he has the money, get rid of him. You know what, get rid of him anyway. Twenty large for you."

"Done."

~ * ~

Mat drove to the next block and parked directly in front of the wrong house. He sat for a minute. He decided he didn't want to use his badge to get in. He had to find another way. He looked back at Hector.

He said, "Okay, Hector, slide down. Don't let this guy see you. When he opens the door, take a peak. If he's the guy, give me a thumbs up. I'm keeping the car running. As soon as I get the money, we're out of here."

He got out, walked up and rang the doorbell. The door swung open and a man stood in front of him in a gray sport coat, black pants and a blue striped shirt.

Mat said, "Hello. I would like to speak with you for a minute."

"What? Why? What's this about?"

Mat turned and looked at the car. He could see two thumbs sticking up just above the window. Mat turned back. He was lost for words. He said to himself, *fuck it*. He said, "I am under the assumption that you received a package today at nine a.m. Is that correct?"

Fred could feel the heat scroll through his body. He had to remain cool. He coughed and took a deep breath. "Your assumption is incorrect. Now good-bye."

Mat stuck his foot to block the door, then pushed it open with his right hand. Fred stumbled back. Mat stepped into the house. Fred cried out, "I don't know what you're talking about. You have the wrong house."

"Let me make this as easy and simple as possible. This morning at eight you answered the door. A Mexican man came in here, took off his shirt, dropped his pants to his knees, ripped a lot of tape off his body and a silky like suit filled with two million dollars dropped to the floor. You signed this piece of paper." Mat threw the paper at him. "And now I want it. Is that simple and easy or what?"

Fred's whole body seemed to be on fire. He let the paper bounce off him. He had to think of something. It was obvious the man standing in front of him knew everything. Denying would not work. Nothing came to mind.

He took a breath and rubbed his hand over his mouth. He decided to give it one last try. He said, "I don't know what the hell you're talking about. No Mexican came to this house. I've been here alone all morning."

Mat slid closer to Fred and grabbed his collar. He pushed his face up to Fred's. He snarled, "Jesus, man. I don't want to hurt you. Don't be stupid. He was here. We both know it. Just give me the money and I'm on my way and none of this happened."

Fred could hardly breathe. He stammered, "Okay...okay. It happened like you said. It didn't take me long to figure the Mexican was at the wrong house. For sure it had something to do with a drug deal. Hell, I'm a businessman, for Christ sake. I did what any other good citizen would do; I took the money to the police."

Mat pushed him away and laughed. He didn't want to show his badge, but he figured he had no choice. The man had the money and this was his chance to get it. "What's your name?"

"Fred."

"So, Fred, you took the money to the station. Right?"

Fred stuttered, "Right...yes...to the station."

Mat looked around the room. He spotted a couple of suitcases in the corner. "And the two suitcases and the fancy clothes you're wearing mean nothing. Well, to me it means you're getting ready for a trip."

"Yes, my wife and I are going away for the weekend."

"It's Tuesday."

Fred was lost. His mind was scrambled. He didn't know what to do or say. He just stood there.

Mat continued, "Now, one more time. Is the money in one of the suitcases?"

Fred stood firm. He had to stay with his story. "I said I took the money to the police station."

Mat yanked back his jacket. His badge was attached to his belt. He pulled it back more to reveal his weapon in the holster. "See this... look. I am the police. Believe me I would have known that two million dollars showed up at the station. And if you brought the money this morning, you'd still be there in the interrogation room. I know about this. Like I said, I am a cop. Now, I don't want any trouble. Which suitcase holds the cash?'

"You're a cop? Why didn't you say so when you knocked on the door... wait... wait...you're no cop. That's a bogus badge. If you were a cop you would have arrested me right away. You're after the money."

Mat slid closer to Fred. He leaned forward. "Listen to me. I got a tip the money was to be delivered to a house on this street. You were right; it was delivered to your house by mistake. The street numbers were transposed by...why the hell am I telling you this? Give me the fucking money or go to jail."

Fred stood firm. He had the feeling something wasn't right. He snapped back, "What if I don't?"

"Don't do this to yourself. If you hand it over, there won't be a problem. I walk out of here as if you did nothing wrong. Screw with me and you go down hard."

Fred stepped back. "Something isn't right. You're not here on police business. You're here to grab the money for yourself. I—"

Mat took a few steps back and smiled, "Fred, Fred. I didn't want to tell you this, but this is an undercover sting operation. Our team has been on the street waiting for the dropoff. So, we were at the right house which now we know was the wrong house. Our team found the Mexican who dropped...you know what? Enough of this. Open the suitcases. Now."

Fred was confused. For some reason, he still didn't believe the story. "I see it. Once I give you the money, you're going to have to kill me. Kill me because you'll be afraid, I'll call the police and tell them some cop took the money."

"You're not getting this. I am the police. I control this. I don't care if the money was delivered here by mistake. All I know is that the money was delivered here. I know this because I already told you I arrested the Mexican a short time ago. You're killing me."

"Maybe...maybe not."

"Oh, Jesus. Now, I must tell you the whole story. I get a tip a businessman is running drugs to make ends meet. Hey, it's a tough economy out there. The tip was right. So I guess you are that businessman."

Fred shouted. "No! I'm not into drugs. Okay. But..."

Mat shouted, "Ah, Jesus, man...why all this bullshit? We're running out of time. I make the call and soon there will be a SWAT team here and you'll be at the station trying to explain all this. Nobody is going to believe you and this wrong address bullshit. Give me the money. I walk away and it's all over."

Fred knew it was over. "And you're not going to kill me...right?"

"Stop it. I just want the money and put an end to this. Plus, I'll get a citation for a job well done. Let me say this one more time. The money was delivered to the wrong house, okay? I tracked down the Mexican. He showed me his GPS. He transposed the last two numbers. Now, I am offering you a deal. You're an innocent bystander. Give me the damn money and your name is never mentioned. Fuck with me and the entire police force will be here, tear this house apart and take you downtown. Why in the hell can't you get this? Plus, I said it is a sting operation. If I have to bring in the troops, it becomes national news and the whole sting is ruined."

Fred smiled and said, "Maybe we can work this out. Maybe throw a couple grand my way and no one will miss it. And I won't tell anyone you were here and took the money."

Fred's face showed he still thought it was a bunch of lies. But he figured it was a way to get some of the money and forget it ever happened. He said, "I can be trusted."

"I'm running out of patience with you. Just get the fucking money and shut up."

Fred took a deep breath and said, "Come on, at least think about it."

"Give me the money first. And you know what, I'll make it worth your time."

Mat figured if he gave him the money he asked for, he would be sure the man would forget the whole thing and he'd get some cash.

Fred said, "The money isn't in the suitcases. Follow me."

Mat pulled his Glock from his holster and followed him down the long hallway.

Forty

Sue took the short walk down the quiet street and entered the house. She walked back in the kitchen and stood there staring at Charlie. He looked up. "You're back. Are you going to cut me loose?"

"Maybe."

"Come on. What's up?"

"It seems you were telling the truth. You won't believe this, but the money was delivered to a house a few blocks away. The Mexican punched in the wrong numbers in a GPS."

"Who gives a shit? Just cut me loose."

Sue found a knife and walked toward him. She leaned over and smiled. "This never happened, right? So, don't get all pissy on me and think about calling the cops."

"Now why would I do that?"

Sue began to cut off the tape. He looked at her. "You think maybe you could, you know, do your little act again?"

She didn't respond. She finished cutting him loose. He leaped up and stretched and twisted his body around.

"Well, I'll be going. I guess this little fuck up cost you fifty big ones," she said.

"I guess."

"Whatever. Here's two hundred. Enjoy." She tossed the money on a table.

Sue started toward the front door. When she reached for the doorknob, she felt Charlie's hand grab her arm. She turned toward him and saw a gun pointed at her. "Two hundred dollars? Are you kidding me? Take me to the house. Now."

"What the hell are you taking about?'

"I deserve that money. I've been tied up for hours. Wrong house. Right house. It doesn't matter. If the money is down the street, the hell with everybody. I want it all."

Before Sue could respond, he pushed her toward the door. Sue shouted, "Wait. Listen to me first. The guy who was here. Mat. He's with the El Paso police. You walk in that house with a gun on me and you're dead meat. Besides, he's my man."

"Come on. You're stalling. He ain't no cop. Let's go. You're so full of it."

"Charlie, you don't want to take that chance. There's a lot going on you don't know about. Mat's going to get the money and take it to Fat Baby. You try to mess this up and you'll be arrested as part of a drug deal gone bad. Mat can make it happen. Your name's in the paper because you'll be dead. And not by him, but by Fat Baby himself."

"You're telling me the guy who punched me out and kicked me in the ribs is a cop and he's picking up the money for the fat man. If that's the case, he's a bad cop. I'm going to mess him up."

"Charlie...Charlie listen to yourself. Don't be making up shit. You should use common sense on this one. You don't want to get involved in this. He's tough, mean and will not hesitate to blow you away." Sue whispered, "Damn, I wasn't supposed to say anything. But this is a sting operation. You screw this up and everybody's going to get screwed. He will easily end your life as part of the drug deal. Fat Baby goes to jail and you go six feet under."

"Even if I use you as a shield? See, I walk down there with you ahead of me. He gives me the money and I'm gone."

"You're not listening to me. Your greed is messing with your head. You keep forgetting you were to give the money to me and Mat. If you take the money from Mat, well, it sounds like you're not going to deliver it to Fat Baby. And Mat tells Fat Baby you took the money and you'll have half of Mexico after you...not to mention the entire El Paso police force. I'm thinking you'll be dead before you can even sniff the money. Or, if you kill us, you'll have every policeman in the world looking for you. You got that in you, Charlie?"

Charlie thought for a second. He said, "Maybe I get the money, take my fifty grand, and I give the money to Fat Man. Huh? How's that sound? Now, move it."

"Listen to yourself. Remember the plan. Mat was to pick it up. Then it was me. You said yourself Fat Baby told you a woman was making the pickup. Do you even know where to deliver the money?"

Charlie stared at her for a minute. He stammered, "I'll...I'll hold the gun to your head, get the money and tell your pal to give me Fat Boy's address."

Sue continued, "If we go down there with a gun to my head, he is not going to believe all you want is the fifty grand. He will shoot you."

"But I want my share."

"Okay...okay. I think that's fair. I can make it work. When he gets the money, we'll be back with your share."

"And I can trust you?"

"It's part of the deal. Fat Baby promised you. I know all about this trust shit. Mat knows that. But if you go down there waving a gun, all hell is going to break out. And you'll end up with nothing...or dead. My word is all you got."

"But you said he was your man. If I have a gun to your head, he will hand over the money to me."

"Again, you're not thinking straight. I know what will happen. Both of you will have guns out. Yours will be pointing at my head. Mat's will be pointing at you. He won't give in. What are you going to do? Shoot me? Then he will shoot you. You're dead."

"But he won't let me shoot you."

"You're not getting this. For two million big ones, he might shoot me...then you."

"I don't know."

"Okay, this is nuts. Think this out. You are going to walk down the street with a gun pointed at me. You won't be pointing at my head. Probably under your shirt. I will kick you in the nuts and run. Oh, you're going to shoot at me. The neighbors will like that."

He took a step back. He released his grip on Sue. She quickly turned and trotted away. Charlie watched as she made her way to the car. She stopped and said, "I will return with your money. It's all in the deal. Fat Baby is happy, you'll be happy. And, oh, and alive."

He watched her walk away. He decided to wait a few minutes and work his way to the back of the wrong house to see what was going on.

~ * ~

Bone and his partner pulled out of the parking space and drove down the street. He looked over and said, "I got to believe the man was telling the truth. He never got the money."

"The Mexican took it and never delivered it," his partner said.

"We'll wait for Fat Baby's call." He paused. Out of the corner of his eye he spotted a car. He yelled, "Holy shit."

"What?"

"That car. The old Mustang. It belongs to a cop I give a few bucks to each week. Fat Baby pays him off. He must have used him to pick up the money. I'm going to follow him and let's see what's he doing here."

They watched as Mat pulled up in front of the house. The car stopped for a few minutes, then continued down the street. They saw him stop at a house a few blocks away.

"Something's going on." Bones swung the car around and drove slowly down the street, keeping a safe distance behind Mat. He grabbed his cell and called Fat Baby. He said, "I just saw that cop, Mat, go into a house. It isn't the house where the money was supposed to be delivered. Is he the pickup?"

"First, yes. And what the fuck are you talking about?"

"He pulled up in front of the house with the address you gave me. He never got out of the car but drove a few blocks to another house on the same side of the street."

Fat Baby didn't need much time to figure out what had happened. "It looks like Hector got screwed and took the money to the wrong house. Get down there but don't let Mat see you. Observe and report. If that's the case and Mat gets the money, you follow him to make sure he delivers the money to me. I'm beginning to lose faith in trusting people. Now it's different. Now it's fear. If any one of the people involved gets a notion to take the money and run, I will find that person and blow a hole in his head wider than the Rio Grande. You got it?"

Bones stammered, "I...I got it, boss."

Forty-one

The two Mexicans followed Mat as he turned onto El Camino Real. They continued a few feet, then pulled over and stopped. They watched as Mat pulled up in front of a house. They saw him stop the car, wait a few minutes and then proceed down the street. They followed him, paying no attention to the other car that was parked a few houses away.

Bones and his partner watched as Mat entered the house. Bones looked down the street. He saw a cross street. He started the car and drove past two houses and turned to the right. He parked the car and said, "Let's go. Around the back."

The two men walked behind the house on the corner and worked their way toward the back of the house. Bones said, "God, this whole neighborhood is so fucking quiet. Jesus, anybody live in these houses?"

"They're all at work."

"Let's see if we can get in the back and see what's going down."

Bone and his partner slipped open a latch to a small gate and walked into a small back yard. They ducked down and worked their way to a large sliding glass door and looked inside. They saw Mat and other man talking.

~ * ~

The two Mexicans sat in the car. "I bet he's here to pick up the money," one of them said.

"Let's call it our money."

"You thinking what I'm thinking?"

"What the hell. Let's do this. I could give a shit about The Captain. He pays us shit and he's driving around in his fancy car. Big house. It's our turn."

"We'll need to get the money and get out of town fast."

"Right to the airport and a flight to Mexico City. I got good friends there and we can get lost for sure."

"Sounds like a plan. Let's go make it happen."

The two Mexicans got out of the car and walked briskly toward the house. They paid no attention to the Mustang in front of the house. Sue saw them and ducked down and watched as the men approached the front door. She turned around and said, "I don't like this. They're Mexicans. They're going in after the money. We need to warn Mat. Come on."

Hector called out, "Not me. You got the gun. I'm staying right here."

Sue waited until the men threw open the door and vanished into the house. She quickly exited the car and jogged toward the open front door.

~ * ~

Mat followed Fred into the garage. He watched as Fred pulled back a few cabinets and reached inside a large hole. Mat stepped closer and pointed his weapon at Fred. "What the hell are you doing?"

"The money," Fred stuttered, "It's...the money...here. I hid it in here."

Mat watched as Fred pulled out the suitcase. He said, "Let's get back into the house."

Mat followed Fred as he walked down the long hallway and into the bedroom. He opened the case. Mat smiled as he saw the money wrapped neatly in bundles.

Mat began counting out some of the bills. "Here is your money. Two hundred thousand like we agreed. Now, do you have a sports bag? I don't like this bulky suitcase."

Fred took a deep breath. "Yes. I'll get it."

Mat waited as Fred opened the closet and grabbed a red and white sports bag. Mat opened the suitcase and stuffed the money in the bag.

Mat said, "Listen and listen closely. We have a deal. I walk out of here and as far as you're concerned this day never happened. Take the little lady on the weekend trip you had planned."

Fred nodded. Mat walked toward the front door. Bones could see him through the opening and could see him carrying the bag. He shouted, "He's got the money. Let's go." Bones and his partner ran into the house through the open sliding glass door. Mat heard the noise and turned sharply toward the two men. Bones shouted, pointing his weapon at Mat. "Drop it, Mat. We're taking the money to Fat Baby."

Mat stood firm. He held the bag tightly in his hand. Bones called out again, "Don't be a dead hero. Give it up."

Mat said, "I was hired to get the money and deliver it to Fat Baby. Sounds to me like you have no intention of delivering the money to him."

"You're dead in two seconds, holding the bag or alive with it on the floor."

Mat let the bag drop out of his grip. Bones took a few steps toward him when shots rang out, making it sound like a Fourth of July fireworks display. Bones or his partner didn't see the two Mexicans who had entered the house. The Mexicans didn't hesitate. They opened fire. Bones was hit in the stomach and dropped to the floor. His partner got a bullet in the chest but was able to fire off two rounds before he fell to the floor. One of the Mexicans felt a bullet hit his chest, right below his heart. His body slumped to the floor.

Mat acted instinctively and dove to the floor. He yanked his weapon from his holster and fired wildly in the air in the direction of the lone standing Mexican. The Mexican dropped behind a sofa and reloaded his weapon.

Fred had started to walk into the living room when he heard gunfire. He acted immediately and ran as fast as he could back into the bedroom. He stopped for a second trying to collect his thoughts. He looked around the room and decided the best exit from the house was through the bathroom. He grabbed his money, scampered into the bathroom and locked the door. He ripped off the screen of the window and smashed it open with the lid from the toilet. He stood on the toilet seat, crawled out the window and ran as fast as he could behind the house and down through the maze of back yards.

Sue reached the front door when she heard the shots. She didn't hesitate She ran through the open door. She looked in and saw one of the Mexicans squatting behind a sofa. The other Mexican was lying in a pool of blood on the floor. She watched as the other Mexican raised up and looked around the room. He didn't see her as she moved quietly into the large living room.

She spotted Bones as he tried to push himself up. She watched as he stopped for a second and fell back on the floor. His partner knelt on one knee trying to collect himself. He tried crawling across the floor but stopped and rolled over. The pain was shooting through his body and he could see the blood seeping out of the bullet wound. He tried to keep from passing out. He took deep breaths and tried to get up. He couldn't make it. He dropped back onto the floor.

Mat crawled across the room trying to find a safe place when the Mexican saw him, raised up, fired his weapon and hit Mat in the side. He yelled and rolled over. The Mexican saw Mat hit the floor and walked over and stood over him. He aimed his weapon to finish him off. He smiled. "Nice try, gringo. I'm taking the money."

Sue was behind him. She raised her weapon, wrapped both hands around the handle. She didn't hesitate. She took aim and pulled the trigger three times. The bullets struck the Mexican in the back. He screamed out and fell to the floor.

Sue could hear the sirens in the distance. She figured someone had heard the gunshots and called 911. Bones' partner tried to stand up and raise his weapon toward her, but the pain and loss of blood caused him to fall back. Sue looked around feeling the silence. She figured either everybody was dead or hurt too badly to move. She was ready to call for Mat when she saw the red and white sports bag. She had to believe the money was in the bag. Again, she didn't hesitate. She ran across the floor, grabbed the bag, threw it over her shoulder and bolted toward the glass sliding door.

Mat knew he was losing blood. He tried to focus. The shooting had stopped. He tried to raise himself up. He reached for the arm of the chair but dropped back down. He heard a noise and turned over. He could see someone moving but his vision was blurry. He could see colors flash by. Red and white. It was the bag with the money. He felt like he was going to pass out. He kept telling himself to hold on.

Sue ran out through the opening and out the open gate to the house next door. She found a side door that led into the garage. She tried to open it. It was locked. She fired her gun at the door and the handle went limp. She pushed it open and raced into the dark garage.

Two police cars pulled up and several officers hurried into the house. They yelled out, "El Paso Police. No one move." Nobody did. One of the police officers used his cell and called for backup and ambulances.

Mat rolled over and called out. "Over here. I'm Mat Watkins, El Paso Police. I'm hit. There are four people in here. All of them have been hit. Be careful. Check them out."

One of the officers found one of the Mexicans bloody and lying still. The other officer checked the other Mexican. He was dead. The other officer called in, "Officer down. Please respond."

Bones was coming around. He didn't move. The officers found him and his partner and took control of their weapons.

Mat sat up. One of the officers came over to him. He said, "Here... my badge on my belt."

"I know who you are."

"I'm hit in the side. I'm bleeding, but I'll make it."

"Hold on. I called for backup and an ambulance."

Mat closed his eyes and laid back down. The officer asked, "What the hell went on here?"

"I got a tip on a drug deal. I came in late. The shooting started, and I took a hit."

Mat held on to a chair and pulled himself up. He looked around. The sports bag was gone. An image of Sue flashed into his mind. It was her. She shot the Mexican and took the money.

He tried to work his way toward the front door. He looked outside. The Mustang was still there. He reached for the doorknob. He couldn't make it. He felt the pain, saw only darkness and passed out. He didn't feel a thing as he bounced off the hardwood floor.

Fred kept running down the street. One of patrol cars spotted him and pulled the car in front of him. Fred stopped. One of the policemen jumped out of the car and pointed his weapon straight at him. He yelled, "Hands on your head and hit the ground."

Fred did what he was ordered to do.

Forty-two

Charlie decided to take a chance. If Mat was a cop, then he was a bad cop. He figured that if he took the money from him, he couldn't do anything about it. He tucked his weapon in his waist, calmly opened his front door and began to take a step out when he heard the sirens. He jumped back into the house and slammed the door. He looked out the window to see several squad cars roar down the street. All he could think about was that the little quiet street in El Paso wasn't quiet any longer. He ran to his office, opened his safe and took out a bundle of money. He found his ticket to Las Vegas, grabbed his suitcase and headed to the garage. In a few minutes, he backed out of the driveway and was on his way to the airport. His whole body trembled as he drove out of the neighborhood. All he could think about was he would not be returning to 11646 El Camino Real for a long, long time; maybe never.

~ * ~

Sue looked around the dark garage and saw the button for the automatic garage door. She looked out the window. Two ambulances had arrived along with two more cop cars. She waited for everybody to go into the house. The street looked empty. She pressed the button and the garage slowly rose. She took a deep breath and grabbed the bag. She walked toward the red Mustang. A police officer appeared from the side of the house. She took a second to compose herself. She was no longer Sue, but Divine, the dancer, the actress. She turned her head toward the garage and called out, "I'll call you from the airport, dear."

She turned back toward the officer, smiled at him and kept walking. He stopped and glanced at her. She said calmly, "I heard some sounds coming from that house there. I'm on my way to the airport to catch a flight. What's going on?"

"I just arrived. I'm going in."

"I'll have to call my husband later and find out what the hell happened in there."

She turned and walked toward the car. She didn't know what to expect. The officer called out, "Have a nice flight."

She breathed a sigh of relief, opened the door and threw the bag in the back seat. Hector had rolled on the floor and curled up in a fetal position. She pulled the gear shift into drive and drove slowly down the street. She looked over and saw the police had someone lying on the ground. She kept on driving. No one noticed her. She was on her way to the Ford dealership. Her only concern was what to do with Hector. She found a gas station, pulled in and stopped the car. She turned around, "Hector, take some of the money and count it out."

Hector ripped open the zipper. He grabbed a stack of money. He counted. He yelled out, "I got a stack. Ten thousand."

"Take another ten and I'm going to let you out."

Hector fumbled around in the case and grabbed another stack. He put it in his pocket and crawled out of the car. He ran as fast he could down the street. Sue drove away and couldn't wait to buy her new Mustang and get out of El Paso.

~ * ~

Hector Morales was a wreck. He had found a bar and called a fellow worker. He told him his truck had broken down and he needed a ride home. The man declined at first, but Hector begged and then offered him a thousand dollars. The man followed Hector's direction and was there within the hour.

Hector called his house. He knew his wife would be there. She answered. He said, "Listen to me and do not ask any questions. Just do as I say. Call your sister and have her come pick you up. Go to the school and get the children. And go to her house. I will be there in a couple hours."

His wife began to speak. "Hector—"

"Stop. Just do it now. Go. Hurry. Please go. I will explain later."

Two hours later, Hector and his family were traveling to a small fishing village to stay with a friend until he figured what the hell he was going to do. He had gone too far and now he had to worry about what would happen to him and his family.

~ * ~

Fat Baby couldn't believe nobody was calling him. He tried Mat's phone. He didn't answer. He called Bones. He didn't answer either. He knew someone had taken the money. But who? Could it have been Hector? Or Mat? Or Bones? Or maybe his trusted accountant?

It wasn't the money that bothered him; it was the fact someone had betrayed his trust. The only thing he cared about was people trusting him and he would offer trust in return.

He couldn't wait any longer. He called for his driver and two of his men. He decided to drive to his accountant's house. He wanted to find out first-hand who the thief was and who had betrayed him.

The limo turned onto El Camino Real and stopped in front of Charlie's house. Fat Baby couldn't see out of the darkened windows. He couldn't see the half dozen police cars and the two ambulances parked a few houses down the street.

One of his men got out of the car and stood frozen for a second as he saw the drama down the street. He gathered himself and knocked on the back window. The window rolled down. He said, "There's a fucking mess down the street. Cop cars and ambulances everywhere."

"What the hell do you mean?" Fat Baby asked.

"There must be a half dozen...shit, they're bringing bodies out right and left."

"We need to get out of here."

"Something bad went down. That's for sure."

The man rushed back and jumped into the front seat. The driver began to turn around when a squad car pulled up beside the limo. Two officers slid out of the car and walked toward Fat Baby's car. The driver stopped the limo as one of the officers motioned to the driver to roll down the window. He looked in. "You live on this street?"

The driver responded. "No, sir."

"Why are you here?"

"I got lost. The streets are a maze around here. I made a wrong turn and am turning around."

"Then keep going. We are blocking off this street."

"Gotcha."

Fat Baby sat nervously in the back seat. He relaxed when he heard the conversation. As they drove off , he didn't see the officer write down the license plate of the limo.

Later that night he heard what had happened, on the news. The next morning the police surrounded his mansion and he surrendered peacefully.

<h1 style="text-align:center">Forty-three</h1>

Mat Watkins was a beaten man. The pain was there but it was tolerable. He had been in the hospital for five days. He was to be released in a few hours. For days, he ran through his mind what had happened that day. He read the paper and saw the TV shows reporting the events. There was no mention of Sue or Hector. He knew the blurry figure he saw dash across the room must have been Sue. He couldn't believe she had not contacted him. It was on the news that he had been wounded and taken to the hospital. She knew where he was. She had taken the money and run.

He figured Bones had decided to take him out and take the money for himself. Or maybe Fat Baby had decided he was expendable and saved fifty thousand. Either way he had learned Bones had been wounded and taken to the same hospital. He also saw on the news a man called Fat Baby had been arrested.

He figured the two Mexicans were there protecting their money or maybe to take it for themselves. He had already called his friend at the Ford dealership. He confirmed Sue had bought the car that same day with cash. He then checked with his contact at the Beach View Villas. She had called to confirm she was on her way and to save a room.

~ * ~

The door opened and his boss, Captain Ramirez, and two police officers entered the room. Mat felt a different kind of pain flash through his body. He could tell by the look on his boss's face that something was wrong.

The captain spoke first. "How are you feeling, Mat?"

"Good. I'm being sent home today. I'll probably hang out at home for a few days before I report."

"Mat, I'm sorry to tell you but you're under arrest. The district attorney has filed multiple charges against you. There's not much to say except that Fred Cummings used his get out of jail free card and well, he told quite a story. The drug boys finally found Fat Baby. He also had a lot to say."

"You talk to him?"

"No. I learned that he told them what they wanted to hear. There were no drugs to be found and nobody found any money. It's bullshit, but Fat Baby wasn't charged. There was nothing to charge him with. I guess giving you a bribe wasn't what they were interested in. Just the fact *you* took the bribe."

Mat didn't say a word. He knew the best thing to do was to remain silent and as soon as possible hire a good attorney. He knew several who would represent him.

"Officer, read him his rights. Mat, get up and get dressed." He paused. "And get yourself a good lawyer. You're going to need one."

One of the officers read Mat his rights and the other waited until he was dressed, pulled his arms behind his back and put the handcuffs on. The captain left the room and returned in a few minutes with a nurse who pushed a wheelchair toward him. Mat sat and was pushed out of the room, down the hall and out the door. He stood and was pushed into the back seat of the patrol car.

~ * ~

Mat sat across from his attorney. He was dressed in his orange prison jump suit. The lawyer said, "You holding up all right?"

"They got me in a private cell. What's going on?"

"The truth is, well, it's not going too good. The arraignment is Friday. It's not going to go well. I've heard the D.A. and the police commissioner want to make a big deal out of all this. You know, a bad cop taking bribes, withholding evidence, obstruction of justice... should I go on?"

"What's your feeling about getting me out on bond?"

"Not good. The D.A, is going to say you're a risk to run. Plus, because of your criminal activity, you'll be a danger to society."

"That's a bunch of bull. Who am I going to harm?"

"Some guy named Fred."

"So what now?"

"I'll do what I can. I'm asking for a speedy trial. I'm not too sure it's going to happen. They want you to stew in this jail for a long time before the trial. They want to milk this and use you as an example to other cops who think they can take bribes."

"Jesus. Any good news?"

"I was able to get Bones out on bond."

"That's funny. A drug dealer and murderer is out on bond and you're saying I got no chance."

"What can I say?"

Mat thought for a second. He leaned over and said, "Give me a piece of paper and pen."

Mat wrote a note. *'Bones. Get your butt to the Beach View Villas in LaPaz and find that dancer you said was hot. You know who I mean. She's got the money. Leave some for me. I'll need a ton to pay for my defense. And don't try to fuck me over this time.'*

"Give this note to Bones."

The attorney took the note and put it in his pocket. He said, "Just hang loose and let me work this. Just remember; be humble, apologize, tell everyone how greed caused damage to your family and the department."

Mat didn't say a word. He stood and walked back toward the door. He turned around and said, "Work it hard, Counselor. Find something or somebody who can help us."

~ * ~

Sue sat on a lounge chair outside her villa in La Paz. After she dropped Hector off and bought her new car, she hid out in a small motel for several days outside of El Paso waiting to see what was going to be reported. She read the paper and followed the news. Every local station aired the whole story. Even CNN and Fox jumped on the bandwagon. They couldn't get enough of a local cop taking bribes and being caught up in a drug deal. Her name was never mentioned.

She wasn't sure what to do or where to go. She knew everyone would be looking for her. She figured by then Fat Baby had gotten to Hector and he had told him about her. Or that guy Bones, who she remembered from seeing at the club, was for sure looking for her. She knew he was shot but learned by watching the news he was alive and was arrested.

After the story broke that Mat had been arrested, she headed for the villa in La Paz. She figured Mat would be in jail and she could feel safe there for a while until she came up with a plan. Mat had already reserved the room. He had told her it was a quiet place to hide out.

She jiggled her toes in the soft warm sand. She took a long drink of her margarita. She looked over at a tall, lean tan man. She smiled. He smiled back and reached out his hand. She touched it, squeezed and pulled him toward her. They kissed. She threw her head back and laughed out loud, "Enrico, you are one cool dude. Sexy, too."

~ * ~

Betty sat quietly watching the news. Never in her wildest dreams, could she have imagined Mat doing the things he did. Her boss had questioned her, but she was never mentioned in any of the discussions. She reached over, shook her head, and turned off the TV.

Forty-four

Bones drove into La Paz. He called the jail and was able to talk to Mat.

"Looks like you got a heap of trouble in front of you."

"I know. But we're working some deals. We'll see."

"I was surprised by the note. I had to laugh when I read it. You are a trusting soul. You really do believe I would save a few bucks for you."

"You want the truth. Well, I felt like I had no other option. If you find her and if you get the money...what can I say?"

"You know, Mat. I like you. You're a good guy. Too bad about what happened. One question for you: were you really going to give the money to Fat Baby?"

He lied. "I was. I really didn't want to have to look over my shoulder for the rest of my life. The fifty large was good enough for me. And you know Fat Baby and the trust thing, I kind of bought into it. How about you?"

He also lied. "I would have taken the money to him, too."

Mat laughed out loud. "Bones. It's me. Why the fuck would you come into the house, guns drawn? To make sure he got the money. I don't think so...but before you say anything, it's all right. If you wanted to take the chance, then it is what it is."

Bones laughed. "I was ready to run."

"Bones, if you get the money, do what you have to do. I had to take a shot. I need some of that money to get out of this fucking mess."

"You know, Fat Baby is going nuts. He's got every man who works for him looking for the money. As far as the Mexicans are concerned, they have taken over his meth operation. I heard they shut it down. Something about a new drug. Cheap to make and easy money. That's all they care about. The one Mexican who lived was released on bond and is gone. Probably deep in Mexico somewhere."

"Have you talked to Fat Baby?"

"I haven't seen him, nor do I want to. I've been hiding out in New Mexico. He's after me, too. But I think I'll be safe. He'll still have every person he's ever known looking for me, your lady friend and Hector and anybody else he can think of."

"Bones, I talked to the owner; she's at the villa. If you get the money, save me four hundred thousand. I think you'll be fine with a mill plus."

"Tell you what? I'll do it. When I get the money, what do you want me to do with your share?"

"Call me and I'll give you an address to mail it to. Wrap it up like a present and mail it."

"I'll be in touch." The phone went dead. Mat smiled to himself. He thought *I'll never see a penny of that money.*

~ * ~

Bones asked for directions to the Beach View Villas. He found the place and parked a few blocks away. He walked down the street. He looked around and found a path leading to the beach. He went around the back. He noticed the villas had patios that backed up to the beach. He causally strolled down the beach and looked into each villa. He spotted two people sitting in lounges in front of the water. He got closer. He recognized the dancer. He found a beach bar, ordered a beer and waited.

An hour later the dancer stood up, kissed her partner and watched as he walked away. He waited until the man was out of sight. He picked up his pace. Bones jumped up and started toward her. He approached her. He called out, "Hey, you're the dancer from The Pink Lady."

She dropped her glass. She looked at the man and felt an attack of fear she had never felt. She wanted to run but knew there was no place to go.

Bones saw the fear in her face. He said, "Relax. I just want to talk."

Sue couldn't respond. Her mouth wouldn't move. Bones continued, "I'm not here to hurt you. I am here to negotiate. Mat is pissed. He at least expected a phone call."

Sue stammered. "I...I...he was in the hospital. I heard he got arrested. I...I—"

"Sure. I don't give a shit. Just listen. There's enough money to go around. I'll take a million and a half and you can have the rest. Or..."

Sue breathed easier. She wasn't sure if she could believe him. She said, "What money?"

"We got no time for this. Don't be thinking I'm a fool. That I would take the time to find you if I didn't know you had the money."

"You talked to Mat, didn't you? He thinks I took the money, doesn't he?"

"You forgot I was there. I was shot but I wasn't dead. I saw what I needed to see before I passed out. You took the money and ran out of the house."

Sue knew she had been caught. There was no way out of this one. She said, "And you're willing to work out a deal with me. Why would I trust you? As soon as I give you the money, I'm dead."

"A couple of things. I don't need the Mexican police looking for a man who killed a tourist. Plus, I don't know if you have it with you or it's buried somewhere. I take you out and I have nothing. Plus, I am not into torture. I am in a hurry. Don't forget, there are still people looking for the money."

"Like Fat Baby. You still workin' for him?"

"He's out of the picture. Nobody works for him. I'm here to get a share. And like I said, to work out a deal."

"And you're not going to hurt me. Right?"

"We're all thieves. Get it. You did good. You stepped in at the right time and won round one. I believe if everybody gets a share, nobody will feel left out and feel like telling stories or spending the rest of their lives hunting each other down. I would be glad to let you have some and I get some. Cool deal. Right?"

"What's the split again?" Sue asked.

"Let's make it even."

She thought for a second. "There's one million and nine hundred thousand left. I get the mill you get the rest."

"Deal," Bones snapped.

"And you're not going to kill me after I give you your share. Right?"

"Like I just said. It wouldn't make sense to have the police investigating a murder. Who knows if someone sees me talking to you? And shit, I'd be running again and waiting for someone to get me. This way we both get some of the money and move on. You're alive...I'm alive and we're both very rich. We can both hide a long time."

Sue thought for a few minutes. What Bones said seemed to make sense. "Sounds good. Follow me inside."

Bones watched as she disappeared into the back bedroom. She returned with a large soft case. She dropped it on the floor, bent down and unzipped the case. She reached inside and wrapped her finger around the trigger of her .38. She stood and pointed the gun at Bones. She snapped, "Get out. Get out and go tell Mat he's going to jail and I'm going to party, party and party some more."

"Whoa. Put that away."

"Get out. Hear me? Get out."

"What? You going to shoot me? I don't think you will. Christ, you do this and every Mexican cop in town will be here."

"I fucking hope so. A black man breaks into my villa and attacks me. I had to defend myself. You got two seconds to get out. And go back and tell Mat he did this to himself and nobody cares."

Bones backed up. He reached inside his coat for his gun. Sue yelled, "Don't do it. I shot that Mexican in the back and I liked it."

Bones froze. He had to laugh. "At first I thought it was Mat who shot him. I heard a shot before I passed out. I found out later someone shot him. It was you."

"Trust me. It was me. Mat was barely alive. I saved his ass and your ass, too."

"You'll never get away with this. Every Mexican in Mexico wants the money. They don't like being robbed."

"I'll take my chances. Now, get out and don't come around here again. I will not hesitate to put a bullet through your heart. I should do it now but don't need the publicity with you dead and me on the news. Fat Baby will know I have the money. But on the other hand, if you make another move, I will take you down, take off and take my chances."

Bones made a move toward Sue. She raised her arm and said calmly, "I just thought of something. When I shoot you and call the police, I will be able to convince them to keep this private. No press. Two reasons. One, why would they want the news that a black man attacked a white woman in their little resort town? And two, fuck, money talks. Mexican police are noted for...well, you know. Now, get out."

Bones turned and walked out the door. He walked to his car. He drove around the corner and stopped. He had to laugh to himself. *Did that stupid little bitch think I would just leave and go back to El Paso? I got time. I'll hang out until the time is right and no more negotiating. She's dead and the money is mine.*

Two days later an unidentified American female was found floating in the surf. She had been dead for a few hours. Her villa had been broken into and torn apart. The Mexican police said they didn't have any suspects but were working the case as a drug deal gone bad. They had found drugs in her villa. They would cooperate with the American authorities to identify the body and find the person who took her life.

Forty-five

Bones called Mat in jail. "It's over. I've got the money. We're set."

"And her?"

"Gone...for good."

"What a mess. Jesus...I can't believe how things fell apart."

"I'm sending you two hundred thousand. Okay?"

"More than okay." Mat gave him his attorney's address.

"You hear anything?" Bones asked.

"I was denied bail. It's going to be a year before the trial. They got me good."

"I'm in hiding. Nobody will ever find me. Tell the lawyer I won't be around for a trial."

Mat hung up and walked back to his cell. He was to be transported to a federal prison. He had plenty of time to think about the mistakes he had made in his life. About the people he hurt and the people that hurt him. But mainly about how he hurt himself.

Meet Jim Daddio

Jim is retired after a successful career in the business world. He lives in Palm City, Florida with his wife, Jill, of fifty-one years. He has a son, Jimmy Jr, three grandchildren and a daughter, Jennifer.

Other Works From The Pen Of
Jim Daddio

Las Vegas Dead - PI Art Decco travels to Las Vegas to find a runaway teenager. Danielle Augusta is no ordinary teenager. Known as Dani, she is the hottest super model in the world.

Heaven or Hell: A Story of Human Trafficking - A South Florida business man runs an escort business. In order to keep up with the competition, he is forced to smuggle in underage girls from Europe. The girls don't know if they are going to Heaven or Hell.

The Privileged - A wealthy socialite is found murdered by her husband. He immediately becomes a suspect. He proclaims his innocence and hires PI Art Decco to find the real murderer. Art uncovers several people who would want her dead, but in the end, the husband isn't worried. He is rich and one of The Privileged.

Letter to Our Readers

Enjoy this book?

You can make a difference

As an independent publisher, Wings ePress, Inc. does not have the financial clout of the large New York Publishers. We can't afford large magazine spreads or subway posters to tell people about our quality books.

But, we do have something much more effective and powerful than ads. We have a large base of loyal readers.

Honest Reviews help bring the attention of new readers to our books.

If you enjoyed this book, we would appreciate it if you would spend a few minutes posting a review on the site where you purchased this book or on the Wings ePress, Inc. webpages at: https://wingsepress.com/

Visit Our Website

For The Full Inventory
Of Quality Books:

Wings ePress.Inc
https://wingsepress.com/

Quality trade paperbacks and downloads
in multiple formats,
in genres ranging from light romantic comedy
to general fiction and horror.
Wings has something for every reader's taste.
Visit the website, then bookmark it.
We add new titles each month!

Wings ePress Inc.

3000 N. Rock Road

Newton, KS 67114